The
Sound of
Your Voice.

only Really
Far Away

Also by Frances O'Roark Dowell

The Sound of Your Voice, only Really Far Away

Frances O'Roark Dowell

 Atheneum Books for Young Readers
NEW YORK LONDON TORONTO SYDNEY NEW DELHI

atheneum

ATHENEUM BOOKS FOR YOUNG READERS · An imprint of Simon & Schuster Children's Publishing Division · 1230 Avenue of the Americas, New York, New York 10020 · This book is a work of fiction. Any references to historical events, real people, or real places are used fictitiously. Other names, characters, places, and events are products of the author's imagination, and any resemblance to actual events or places or persons, living or dead, is entirely coincidental. · Copyright © 2013 by Frances O'Roark Dowell · All rights reserved, including the right of reproduction in whole or in part in any form. · ATHENEUM BOOKS FOR YOUNG READERS is a registered trademark of Simon & Schuster, Inc. · Atheneum logo is a trademark of Simon & Schuster, Inc. · For information about special discounts for bulk purchases, please contact Simon & Schuster Special Sales at 1-866-506-1949 or business@simonandschuster.com. · The Simon & Schuster Speakers Bureau can bring authors to your live event. For more information or to book an event, contact the Simon & Schuster Speakers Bureau at 1-866-248-3049 or visit our website at www.simonspeakers.com. · Book design by Sonia Chaghatzbanian · The text for this book is set in Lomba Book. · Manufactured in the United States of America · 0713 FFG · First Edition · 10 9 8 7 6 5 4 3 2 1 · Library of Congress Cataloging-in-Publication Data · Dowell, Frances O'Roark. · The sound of your voice, only really far away / Frances O'Roark Dowell. — 1st ed. · p. cm. · Sequel to: The kind of friends we used to be. · Summary: Best friends Marylin and Kate compete for limited school resources when Kate helps her boyfriend seek funding for the Audio Lab, while Marylin covers her interest in the student body president by claiming she only wants his support for new cheerleading uniforms. · ISBN 978-1-4424-3289-5 (hardcover) — ISBN 978-1-4424-3291-8 (eBook) · [1. Best friends—Fiction. 2. Friendship—Fiction. 3. Middle schools—Fiction. 4. Schools—Fiction. 5. Popularity—Fiction.] I. Title. · PZ7.D75455Sou 2013 · [Fic]—dc23 · 2012030308

This book is dedicated to Carla Burkhard, Jennifer Gardner, Mary Beth Lister, Danielle Paul, Suzanne Roberts, Liz Redinbo, and all past and future members of my most marvelous book group. Thank you for ten years of good talk, good books, and good therapy.

Marylin thought she could get away with it. She thought she could be a middle-school cheerleader and a Student Government representative. She thought she could be friends with Mazie Calloway *and* Rhetta Mayes. She thought she could date the Student Government president instead of the captain of the football team, and that would be okay.

Marylin thought she could have it all, and everybody would cheer and clap their hands and be fully supportive, the way people were on TV during the last five minutes of a show.

That was the problem with having two weeks for winter break, she decided later. When you had two weeks off of school, you could believe that life was easy. Life was Christmas trees and hot chocolate and your parents actually sort of getting along when they saw each other. Life was watching TV and getting new clothes, and looking through magazines for different hairstyles that didn't mean cutting your hair. Life was about not caring what people thought, because everybody was doing stuff with their families and didn't have as much time to think about what you were wearing or who you were hanging out with.

Mazie had been out of town for most of the break, and though she texted a lot, it was all about the cute boys at the ski lodge she was staying at. When they were in the same room together, Mazie was always investigating Marylin's life. Why had Marylin been walking down the hall with Jody Reed when everyone knew Jody had to go to speech therapy twice a week? When was Marylin going to get a smartphone? Why had Marylin bought those shoes? Who in the world wore green shoes?

Frankly, it was exhausting. So for Marylin,

the two weeks of break had been like a spa vacation. Sure, she'd met the other middle-school cheerleaders at the mall, and gone to a sleepover at Ruby Santiago's house and another one at Ashley Greer's, but most of the time she'd just hung out at her house or her dad's apartment. As a rule, Marylin didn't find her parents' divorce convenient; in fact, it was the most inconvenient, horrible thing that had ever happened to her. But she had to admit, it gave her a lot of excuses not to do anything that she didn't feel like doing. "I've got to go over to my dad's this afternoon," she'd tell who-ever called—Ruby or Ashley or Caitlin. "But maybe I can hang out tomorrow!"

When she climbed on the bus on the first day after break, Marylin felt refreshed. She was ready for Mazie and Ruby and the other middle-school cheerleaders. She thought she was even ready to tell them that Benjamin Huddle had hiked over to her house one snowy afternoon last week so they could build a snowman together. He'd been so funny and nice, she'd wished she could have texted about him to someone on her new phone, but her friend Kate didn't have a phone, and it was a Sunday, and her friend Rhetta wasn't allowed to use any electronic technologies on Sundays.

Since she was pretty sure Kate and Rhetta were her only friends who would understand the wonders of Benjamin Huddle, all Marylin could do was write in her journal about it later, how snowflakes had gotten tangled up in Benjamin's eyelashes, and how he'd helped her little brother, Petey, build a snowman Albert Einstein. But now, boarding the bus to school, she thought it was time to share Benjamin with the middle-school cheerleaders. They knew she'd gone to the Student Organizations Holiday Extravaganza with Benjamin, after all. How shocked would they be that Benjamin had come over to her house? That she liked him and thought that he was maybe sort of her boy-friend, even though it wasn't official?

Kate was sitting in a seat toward the back of the bus. Marylin slid in beside her and said, "You really need to get a phone. All everybody does anymore is text. Nobody talks."

"I talk," Kate said, sounding stubborn about it. "I like the sound of people's voices."

Marylin sighed. Kate Faber was the most frustrating person on the planet. Marylin and Kate had been friends since preschool, and even if they didn't hang out as much as they used to, well, there was still this bond. But that didn't mean that Kate didn't drive Marylin crazy. Kate was smart and funny, and she'd be cute if she learned how to dress and do her hair, but she seemed to be completely missing the gene that made normal people want to be popular, or to at least fit in. *Of course* Kate didn't text. *Of course* she wore big black clunky boots that made her look like a lumberjack or a fireman. That was Kate's style. Marylin didn't get it at all.

"Well, if you don't care that the whole world is leaving you behind," Marylin said with a shrug.

"I don't," Kate said. "As long as it leaves me my guitar."

Right. The guitar. How could Marylin forget about Kate's guitar? That was another thing.

Somehow last fall Kate had gotten her hands on a guitar, and now she was Miss Rock and Roll. And she was hanging around with this eighth-grade boy named Matthew Holler, who Marylin had to admit was cute, but he wasn't the sort of boy you should hang around with if you got good grades and didn't get in trouble.

As far as Marylin was concerned, there were three kinds of acceptable boys: athletes, student leaders, and select band members, specifically boys who played trumpet or drums. That really gave you a lot of boys to choose from, if you thought about it, even if it excluded boys like Matthew Holler and Sean Kim, who was really cute, but played clarinet and was thereby technically out of the running.

Well, Marylin was not going to get into the topic of Matthew Holler and acceptable boys with Kate. She didn't want to spend her energy on things she couldn't do a thing in the world about. Instead she needed to get focused. She was a middle-school cheerleader and a School Government representative. She was wearing amazing leopard-skin flats she'd bought at Target a few days before, and even though her feet were freezing because you couldn't exactly wear socks with leopard-skin flats, that was okay. Because she had new lip gloss in her back pouch and hummus in a plastic container for lunch, and people liked her and thought she was pretty. All of these things added up to an amazing life. Not a perfect life—she didn't think she could ever have a perfect life, now that her parents were divorced—but a life most girls would envy.

Marylin glanced at Kate, who was leafing through a magazine called *American Songwriter*. Okay, so Kate probably didn't envy Marylin's life. But Kate was—well, Kate. You couldn't expect her to feel things normal people felt. But you could expect her to tell you the truth, and although Marylin didn't always like to hear the truth, she knew that it was good to have a person like Kate in your life.

But one Kate was enough. One would definitely do the trick.

Over the holidays, Marylin had started writing a novel. She'd gotten inspired by a movie she'd watched at her dad's apartment on New Year's Day. It was about a girl who was abandoned deep in the woods with her little brother, who was deaf, and their dog, a golden retriever named Trevor. The girl and her brother had been camping with their mom and stepdad, and one morning they woke up to find themselves alone except for Trevor. They had to figure out on their own how to get home, and how to survive along the way.

Marylin had been sitting on the couch with Petey, a blanket spread across their laps, a gigantic bowl of popcorn between them. She didn't think she'd enjoy the movie; she'd never been camping and was pretty sure she'd hate it—too many bugs—and as a rule, she preferred romantic movies to adventures. Really, if it hadn't been for Trevor the dog, she would have tried to convince Petey to watch something else. But Trevor was so cute, and Marylin had always wanted a dog, so she decided to give *Alone in the Woods* a chance.

By the time it was over, she couldn't wait to start writing. That happened to her a lot with movies; if she really liked the story, it made her want to come up with a story of her own. Her idea was to write a novel about a girl who had been abandoned by her parents, only in a sub-urban neighborhood, not in the woods. Marylin's story would start on the morning after the parents left, with the girl, a seventh grader, waking up and calling out, "Mom, do you know what I did with my history binder?" But her mom didn't answer, because her mom wasn't there, and neither was her dad. It was just the girl, who Marylin decided would be named Christina, because Marylin had always loved the name Christina, and her little brother, Curtis.

Marylin found a yellow legal pad in her dad's desk drawer and took it to her room. It was ten thirty, and she was supposed to have her lights out by eleven, but when she finally looked up from her writing, the clock on her bedside table said one fifteen. She'd written fourteen pages. Christina and Curtis had just found the note their parents left them, saying they were getting divorced and needed some time to themselves. They were sure the children would be fine without them, the note said—there was plenty of food in the kitchen, and they'd left a hundred dollars in the junk drawer—and one of them would be home soon to explain more.

Marylin knew she should turn out her light and go to sleep. In fact, she was surprised her dad hadn't tapped on her door and told her it was way past her bedtime. But there was no way she could fall asleep. She was so mad at the parents in her story she felt like there were ants crawling through her veins. How could they do that to their kids? Just leave them alone with hardly any explanation at all?

In the movie, it had been the evil stepfather who had convinced the children's mother to abandon them. In Marylin's story, abandoning their kids, at least temporarily, was something both parents agreed to do. They couldn't agree about anything else, but they could agree that the kids weren't as important as their own happiness.

The next day she'd called Rhetta and read to her what she'd written so far. Rhetta had been quiet for a few moments after Marylin had finished, and then said, "It's really good, but I'm not sure people will believe that Christina's parents would actually abandon their children. I mean, that's a pretty radical thing to do."

Marylin had thought about this for a minute. "Maybe this is the kind of story that only divorced kids will understand," she said finally.

"Maybe," Rhetta agreed. "Only, Marylin, your parents didn't abandon you. They just sort of abandoned each other."

Marylin found herself nodding fiercely at the phone. "It's exactly the same thing," she said, her throat tightening. "That's what nobody gets. It's exactly the same."

Marylin had planned to spend the rest of the day working on her story, but when she sat down to write, she couldn't figure out what should happen next. She was trying to write a scene with Christina and Curtis in the kitchen before school. Christina wanted to make a special breakfast for Curtis, waffles and bacon, but she realized she didn't know how to use the waffle iron, and she'd never fried bacon before.

That's okay, Curtis told her. *I just want cereal anyway.*

For some reason, that was as far as Marylin could get, Christina and Curtis sitting at the breakfast table, eating bowls of Special K. Every time she tried to make one of them say something or do something, they wouldn't. They just sat there staring at each other, putting one spoonful of cereal into their mouths after another.

This is stupid, she'd finally decided. Rhetta was right. No one would believe that parents would abandon their children like that. Besides, it was depressing. Marylin had no interest in being depressed. She wasn't a depressed sort of person. She was, she decided after thinking about it for a few minutes, the sort of person who needed new shoes.

She stuck her head out of her door and looked down the hall. "Dad? Can you take me to Target?"

"Sure, hon," her dad called back from the dining room. "Let me just finish this e-mail."

When she'd gotten home, she'd started a

new story in her notebook, one about a middle-school cheerleader who had to decide between three boys who all had major crushes on her. This is the sort of story I should be writing, she'd told herself, glancing happily at her new leopard-skin flats. Nobody likes depressing stories, anyway.

Walking down Hallway B of Brenner P. Dunn Middle School, Marylin could tell something was wrong the minute she got within twenty-five feet of Ruby Santiago's locker. All the middle-school cheerleaders were there, Ruby at the center, Mazie by her side, everyone oohing and aahing over all the Christmas booty, the new sweaters and earrings, the makeup kits. Other kids stood around the edges of the circle, wannabe insiders, oohing and aahing along with the cheerleaders, who naturally ignored them. As she got closer, Marylin put on her best middle-school cheerleader smile. She ran her hand through her hair. Here we go, she told herself. The beginning of an amazing new semester.

At that moment, Ashley Greer turned and saw Marylin approaching. Her expression immediately changed. One second Ashley was smiling and acting like Mazie's new palette of eye shadow was the most interesting thing in the world. The next second she looked like a jackal who had just come upon a wounded rabbit in the forest. Marylin's stomach lurched. Ashley's expression, she knew, was not a good sign.

"Look, it's Mrs. Huddle!" Ashley exclaimed to the other cheerleaders, who all turned in Marylin's direction at the same time, like they were a single organism, or a collection of puppets all connected to the same string.

So they knew. Okay, well, so what? Marylin kept the smile plastered on her face as she got to Ruby's locker. Benjamin Huddle was a perfectly respectable boy. More than respectable! He was cute. He was a student leader. So maybe his wardrobe could use a little work. Marylin already had planned to make a few, very subtle suggestions that over time would take care of that problem.

"Oh, stop!" she squealed at Ashley in her

best cheerleader squeal voice, a voice that said, *I know you're only teasing me because you love me so much.* "I am not Mrs. Huddle. We're not even—a thing. Not yet, at least."

"Not now, not ever," said Mazie, taking a step toward Marylin. "We're a geek-free squad, didn't you know that?" She grabbed Marylin by the elbow. "Now come with me. We need to talk."

Which was how Marylin found herself being dragged down the hallway to the girls' bathroom by the library. "You're hurting my arm!" she complained to Mazie, trying to pull free. But Mazie just held on tighter.

"You're hurting my life," she said through gritted teeth. "Now come on."

There were two girls in the bathroom combing their hair, but one look from Mazie sent them scrambling to the door. Mazie led Marylin over to the row of mirrors and turned her around so that Marylin was facing her own reflection.

"Look at yourself," Mazie commanded. "Do you see who you are? You're one of us. And we do things a certain way. We wear certain clothes and have certain boyfriends, and we do things the way we're supposed to do them. What about that do you not get?"

"I—I get it," Marylin replied limply. "Didn't you notice my shoes?"

Mazie looked at Marylin's shoes. "Yeah, okay, so you get the clothes part. Good for you. Glad you can get one thing right. But you're getting the people part wrong. I know you're all sort of 'friendly girl' and 'Miss Nicey-Nice,' and that's okay up to a point. But it's like you'll talk to anyone. And actually be friends with anyone. It's like you don't get it. You're special. *We're* special. And I hate to tell you this, but Ruby is really getting freaked out by you."

Marylin paled. Ruby's opinion, as Marylin and Mazie both knew, was the one that mattered. If you were in with Ruby, every door you walked past automatically opened. Athletes spanning the spectrum of sports from football to track and field thought you were cute. Teachers you'd never had a class with smiled and waved at you in the hallway. The janitorial staff kept the door to your locker extra shiny.

And if you were out with Ruby, you were in Siberia. You simply ceased to exist.

A tiny voice piped, *Who cares?* into Marylin's ear. It was Kate's voice, and it was so clear that Marylin looked around to see if Kate was there. She checked under the stalls for Kate's boots. But no Kate, only her annoying little voice inside Marylin's head. Marylin supposed that was what happened when you'd known someone almost all your life. You got their opinions whether they were in the same room with you or not.

Well, easy for Kate to say. Kate could say, *Who cares?* because she meant it. Or at least sort of meant it. Marylin couldn't believe that Kate didn't really care at all. She was just better at hiding it than most people.

But Marylin cared. She'd always known that about herself. Had always been one hundred percent honest with herself about the fact that she cared. She cared a lot. She cared that people thought she was pretty, and that they thought she was nice. She cared about being popular. She wished that people understood it was hard work being popular! Being popular meant you had to care about everything—how you looked, what you said, who you said it to, and what they thought about it later. You had to pay attention to every little detail.

Marylin stared at her reflection. What had she been thinking? How in the world had she thought she could have it all? Where had she gotten the idea she could be popular *and* have a boyfriend who didn't meet Ruby Santiago's approval? That she could be friends with Rhetta Mayes, who dressed all in black and was always drawing in an oversize sketchbook and would probably pierce her nose the minute she could find someone to do it for her?

But Rhetta's your friend, Kate's tiny voice whispered in her ear. *You've spent the night at her house. She gets you. She makes you laugh.*

Marylin shook her head. She would figure out what to do about Rhetta. Maybe they could just be school friends. They had almost every class together, after all; it wasn't like they never saw each other. And Marylin's schedule was about to get very busy with basketball season starting up. She probably wouldn't have time to hang out with Rhetta after school anyway. And Rhetta would understand.

No she won't, whispered Kate's tiny voice.

Marylin took a deep breath. Rhetta would understand, she repeated to herself. Maybe she could encourage Rhetta to sign up to do makeup for the spring musical, and then Rhetta would be really busy too.

That was it. No problem. Marylin smiled at herself in the mirror. Her smile looked fake, but it would have to do. Now all she had left was the problem of Benjamin Huddle. One of his incisor teeth was just a tiny bit crooked in a way that Marylin totally loved. Could she really give that up? Or the lopsided way he grinned at her. Was she willing to sacrifice that grin just to stay popular?

Sadly, Marylin knew the answer. It made her want to cry, and it probably meant that deep down inside she wasn't the nice person she thought she was. She was only nice on top.

It's because my parents got divorced, Marylin insisted to herself. That's why I need to be popular. I can't help it. It's not my fault.

Yeah, Kate's voice said, this time a whole lot louder. *Right*.

Marylin wished Kate would just shut up. Her life was hard enough without someone making comments about it all the time, even someone who wasn't actually in the same room.

"Tell Ruby not to worry," she told Mazie, reaching into her back pouch for her lip gloss. "I'm fine. I didn't really like Benjamin anyway. I just thought if I went to the dance with him, he might help us get funding for new uniforms."

A knowing look came over Mazie's face, and she smiled at Marylin, nodding. "I thought you were up to something," she said, patting Marylin on the shoulder. "That's why I stuck up for you when Ruby started asking a lot of questions about your so-called friends. 'Marylin's up to something, just you wait,' is exactly what I told her, and I was right. Wow, I bet Benjamin Huddle has no idea he's getting played."

None, Marylin thought miserably as she followed Mazie out of the bathroom. Absolutely no idea in the world.

. . .

"I've got bad news."

Rhetta had turned around in her seat and was now leaning toward Marylin. She didn't look so much like a vampire today. Usually Rhetta was a study in black and white, all black clothes and pale white skin, but today she was actually wearing jeans like a normal person, and although her T-shirt was black, it was a sort of silky-looking V-neck T-shirt that was nice. If only Marylin could make Rhetta see how good she'd look in pink!

"What is it?" Marylin asked, wondering if somehow Rhetta's bad news could be that she'd heard about the conversation Marylin had just had with Mazie five minutes ago in the bathroom.

"I'm grounded," Rhetta said with a dramatic slump so that her chin was now resting on the back of her chair. "For a month, if you can believe it. Just because I rode with Todd Venable to the Quick-E Mart after youth group Sunday night instead of getting a ride straight home with Samantha Werther like I said I would.

Todd brought me home safe and sound, and it's not like he's a psycho killer or anything. He plays drums in the praise band!"

Rhetta's father was a pastor at a local church that was known for being hip and informal. Still, Marylin supposed a drummer in a band was a drummer in a band, even if the band was singing songs about Jesus.

"Did your dad kick Todd out of the band?"

Rhetta shook her head. "No, but he had a long talk with him in his office, which I'm sure was way, way worse. When my dad gives you a lecture, he goes on for, like, ten years."

"Well, I'm sorry you're grounded," Marylin said. "What does that mean exactly?"

As it turned out, it meant exactly what Marylin hoped it meant. For the next month, Rhetta was confined to home except for family outings and church on Sunday, Sunday night, and Wednesday night. "Church is going to be the highlight of my social life for thirty days," Rhetta complained. "How pathetic is that?"

"It could be worse," Marylin said. "They could have kept you home from church, too."

"Right," Rhetta said, rolling her eyes. "That's *so* not going to happen."

Mrs. Clewes started to take attendance, so Rhetta turned back around, and Marylin slid back in her seat, filled with relief. She wouldn't have to make any excuses for a whole month about why she couldn't hang out with Rhetta after school. And who knew what things would be like in a month? In a month, Rhetta's dad might decide to become a missionary to China. And yes, okay, Marylin would miss Rhetta if she moved, but that would definitely solve one of her problems.

And then a thought came to Marylin that was so brilliant she had to stop herself from blurting it out to the whole class. She didn't have to give up Benjamin Huddle, either! Mazie thought she was using Benjamin to get the cheerleaders new uniforms. So she could hang around Benjamin all she wanted. If anybody asked her about it, she'd just mention how cute those uniforms would be if they could just get the funding for them (wink, wink). Ruby and Mazie would totally be on her side. They'd tell her to hang out with Benjamin as much as she wanted!

I am a genius, Marylin told herself, taking out her pre-algebra notebook. I'm so smart I scare myself.

And, much to her amazement, Kate's little voice didn't have a thing to say about it.

In science, Mrs. Patel announced that they would begin the year by studying evolution, and did anyone have a problem with that? Several kids turned and looked at Rhetta because they knew her dad was a pastor, but she just shrugged and said, "Evolution's cool with me."

"Excellent!" Mrs. Patel exclaimed. "I believe seventh grade is a most pertinent time to study Darwin and his ideas about natural selection and the survival of the fittest. Can anyone tell me what that phrase means, 'survival of the fittest'?"

Christof Jenner's hand shot into the air. "Only the strong survive!"

Mrs. Patel nodded. "More or less, that is the theory. And one way the strong survive is by abandoning the weak. Does that sound at all familiar to you?"

Everyone nodded, including Marylin. That really summed everything up, as far as she was concerned. To someone like Kate, Marylin might seem shallow or dumb for wanting to be popular, but it was all about survival. Not everyone could be like Kate, surviving outside the herd. And if you lived inside the herd, well, it was better if you stuck with the strong people, right? If you hung out with the weak, unpopular people, you'd get eaten by wolves in no time flat.

Rhetta raised her hand. "So you're saying that 'survival of the fittest' applies to all animals, even human beings?"

"Yes, but I think that it's complicated," Mrs. Patel said. "Can you tell me what you find troublesome about the idea?"

Rhetta was quiet for a moment before speaking again. "Well, I guess it would bother me because human beings might be animals, but we're also—um, human, if you know what I mean. And we have stuff like morality that tells us we're supposed to protect the weak. Like old people, or disabled people." Rhetta looked around the room and then back at Mrs. Patel. "Does that make sense?"

"Perfect sense," Mrs. Patel confirmed. "And I agree with you. Some people have taken the idea of 'survival of the fittest' to extreme and immoral lengths. But we will discuss the idea in terms of evolutionary science and genetics, and I hope you will find it as fascinating as I do. Now, take out your notebooks, please."

A few students grumbled as they pulled their pencils and notebooks from their backpacks, and Marylin wondered if they'd hoped Mrs. Patel would spend class talking about popular kids versus unpopular kids. Ever since sixth grade, that seemed to be everybody's favorite topic in class discussions. If you were talking about the American Revolution in history, someone would raise their hand and say, "It's like the colonists were the unpopular kids and the British were the popular kids," and then someone else would argue it was the other way around, and then someone else would say that King George was a bully, and by the time you'd worked out who was popular and who was unpopular, the period would be over.

When the bell rang, Marylin followed the herd into the hallway and into the stream of students, where she was jostled and banged into as the faster, more aggressive kids made their way to class. Suddenly she felt an arm draped around her shoulder and looked up to see Will Norton, an eighth-grade football player.

"Let me be your escort," he said, looking down at her with a grin. "It's a jungle out here."

"It really is," Marylin agreed, smiling her best middle-school cheerleader smile, but suddenly she felt nervous, like she had a test she'd forgotten to study for. But that was silly—how could there be a test the first day of the semester? Everything's fine, she told herself. There's nothing in the world to worry about.

She saw Mazie and Ashley walking in her direction, waving and smiling, almost as if they were happy to see her, and Marylin was almost happy to see them—members of her pack, the ones who were going to keep her safe from the wolves. But when Mazie cupped her hand over her mouth and whispered something into Ashley's ear, her eyes trained on Marylin the whole time, Marylin didn't feel safe at all. In fact, she was pretty sure the wolves were a lot closer than she'd thought.

Lorna wanted to try out for the spring musical, but Kate wasn't sure she was the sort of person who tried out for things anymore. She had skipped basketball tryouts in November, because she didn't think basketball went with her black boots or her guitar. She was sort of sorry about it now, especially since her dad worked with Marcie Grossman's mom, and Marcie Grossman played power forward. Her dad was always dropping little tidbits of the girls' basketball team news at dinner, giving Kate pointed looks while he did, like he was saying, *This news should be about you.*

Maybe. Kate couldn't decide. On the one

hand, she missed being around other girls who liked to play basketball, and she missed how she felt after a good game. On the other hand, could you really play basketball and write poetry at the same time? Could you really be the kind of person who was a jock and a guitar player? When tryouts came around, Kate had had a hard time putting the two halves of her life together, and so she decided to pass on basketball this year.

"If we try out for the spring musical, we'll be expanding our horizons," Lorna told Kate in Creative Writing Club while they waited for everyone to get there. "At least that's what my mom says. She's completely freaked out by my life right now because I don't have two million friends."

"You don't need two million friends," Kate said, pulling her poetry notebook out of her backpack. "She knows that, right?"

"But I only have one friend," Lorna said. "Well, let me revise that: I only have one friend in real life, which would be you, by the way. I have hundreds of World of Warcraft friends, but to my mom, they don't count because they're computer friends."

Lorna was obsessed with World of Warcraft and spent most of her Friday and Saturday nights playing it online with ten gajillion other people, although she wasn't friends with all of them, just the ones in her guild. Kate had tried to get interested, but she just wasn't a fantasy person. She liked to be involved with stuff that actually happened with real people or people who could be real if they didn't live in the pages of a book.

"I just don't get why it bugs your mom so much that you only have one close friend," Kate said. "Isn't that better than having ten so-so friends?"

"My mom's deal right now is that all the stuff I like to do is solo—cooking, reading and writing, World of Warcraft," Lorna explained. "Even though World of Warcraft isn't solo. But according to my mom it is, because it's me sitting alone in a room in front of a computer."

Kate waved her arm to indicate the whole of

the classroom. "But this isn't solo. Isn't she glad you're in a club?"

Lorna shook her head sadly. "It's not enough. But if I'm in the musical, that's at least fifty people. And I have to pick one more activity besides Creative Writing Club or I can't do World of Warcraft anymore, so I figure the musical is my best bet, especially if you'll do it with me."

"I don't know," Kate said, doodling a guitar on her notebook. "Can I think about it?"

"The auditions are Friday after school," Lorna told her. "And the sign-up for auditioning ends tomorrow, so you have exactly one day to think about it."

"Okay," Kate said, and then her entire body went electric, which meant that Matthew Holler had entered the room.

To Kate's disappointment, Matthew sat down at a desk on the other side of the room. It seemed to Kate that Matthew was always sitting on the other side of something from her—the cafeteria, the audio lab, and now here. She wished they sat together more, like at lunch or on the wall outside the school's front entrance, where a lot of kids hung out before the first bell or after school waiting for the bus. She knew better than to wish for bigger things, like they'd hold hands when they walked down the hall together. Nobody at Brenner P. Dunn Middle School held hands, not even Marylin and Benjamin, even though everyone knew they were a couple. It was like it was against the law or something.

The last couple of weeks, Kate had had two main thoughts running through her head: Matthew Holler is my boyfriend! Or else, Is Matthew Holler my boyfriend? She really didn't know, although sometimes, like after he'd kissed her behind her garage on the last Saturday of winter break, she was sure the answer was yes. But at other times, like now, when he was halfway ignoring her, Kate didn't know what to think. Was that how a boyfriend was supposed to act? That wasn't how Benjamin acted around Marylin, as far as Kate could tell. He was always sitting with her or making his way through a crowd to get closer to her. Except for the kiss, Matthew pretty much acted the same way to Kate as he always had, which was to say sometimes he seemed really excited to hang out and talk with her, and other times he acted distracted, even kind of mad, when Kate was around, like she was his little sister or something.

The only positive thing Kate could say for sure was that Matthew had broken up with Emily right after Christmas. She knew this because Emily had called her approximately five seconds after it happened to say the breakup was Kate's fault. Since Kate and Emily had only spoken to each other maybe two times in their lives, Kate found this especially weird and sort of stressful, like maybe the next thing Emily was going to do was come over and sock Kate in the face.

"We were fine until you two started hanging out all the time," Emily had complained over the phone. "After that, I wasn't good enough anymore. I didn't play guitar or know all the right bands like Miss Perfect Kate."

Kate had had to choke back laughter. "Are

you serious? You think this is me versus you? Is that even possible? Look at you! Look at me!"

Emily had been quiet for a moment, and then she had said, "Yeah, I know. It's hard to believe. But what else could explain it?"

Kate had kept quiet, although she had a long list of things that might explain it, including the fact that from what she knew from Matthew, Emily was pretty boring, talked about herself all the time, and had never heard of Alex Chilton, Kurt Cobain, or Sufjan Stevens, not to mention a thousand other obscure but crucially important figures of the rock world. Kate and Matthew had a running list of who the most important rock-and-roll innovators of the twentieth and twenty-first centuries were. In fact, Kate's dad told her if she didn't start reading something besides *The Rolling Stone Encyclopedia of Rock & Roll* and *Our Band Could Be Your Life*, he was going to take away her library card so she couldn't check them out anymore, which Kate didn't believe for a second.

That reminded Kate. She took out a sheet of notebook paper and wrote *Quiz* on the top of it. Then she wrote out

Elvis Presley or Buddy Holly?
The Beatles or the Rolling Stones?
Nirvana or Pearl Jam?
Coldplay or the Shins?

When she was done, she carefully folded the paper into a small rectangle and then wrote Matthew's name on it. Passing it to the girl beside her, she whispered, "Pass it down, okay?"

She watched as the note traveled the classroom and landed on Matthew's desk. Matthew unfolded it with one eyebrow raised, as if he were thinking, Hmm, what could this be? As soon as he started reading, a smile broke out across his face, and he grabbed the pencil that was lodged behind his ear and began circling his answers.

Kate looked down at her desk and smiled. Her knowledge of music was the thing she had that no one else had, at least no other girl she'd ever met, and not many other guys, either. Matthew could sit on the other side of the room if he wanted, he could act cool and aloof, but the fact was, this stuff mattered to him as much as it did to Kate. He needed her.

Ms. Vickery rushed into the room. "Sorry to be late! Who brought copies of their work to share?"

The room suddenly filled with the rustling of paper. Lorna leaned over and tapped her pencil on Kate's desk. "Think about it, okay? The musical? It's the only way to save me from my mother."

"I'll think about it," Kate promised, pulling out a sheaf of poems from her notebook. "I'll let you know by tomorrow morning."

But in her head she was thinking, Radiohead or Green Day? Bruce Springsteen or Elvis Costello? PJ Harvey or Pink?

She had a million of 'em.

"Sounds like the boys' basketball team could take a few lessons from the girls this year,"

Kate's dad said at dinner that night. "The girls' zone defense is really working out for them."

Kate nodded. She'd discovered that if she tried to look interested in her dad's basketball reports, he'd drop the topic after a minute or two. Once, she'd made the mistake of rolling her eyes, and he'd gone on for fifteen minutes about the importance of girls' athletics and how girls used to have to wait till high school to play organized sports. Did Kate know that his sister, Tess, had been a great soccer player, which was too bad, since there were no soccer leagues for girls when Tess was growing up?

Kate hadn't rolled her eyes since. She'd thought about trying to explain to her dad that she hadn't given up sports for good, she was just dedicating this year to playing guitar. But she knew he wouldn't like that, either. Kate's guitar playing seemed to make her dad nervous, although he was acting a little more relaxed about it since she'd started playing acoustic. One afternoon last fall when she was still messing around on Flannery's electric guitar, her dad had stood in the doorway to Kate's bedroom and said, "That sounds nice, Kate, but are you sure that's how you want to spend your time?"

Kate had put down the guitar and stared at her dad. "What do you mean?"

Mr. Faber had shrugged. "I don't know, I guess I was just thinking about how we used to spend Saturday mornings playing pickup games over at the Y. You were turning into a good little point guard, Katie. I played guard in high school. I've got a lot more tricks I could teach you."

"It's not like I'm never going to play basketball again, Dad. But right now I want to learn how to play the guitar."

"You could focus on music later," her dad had insisted. "Like when you're old and your knees are shot. You have your whole life to play punk rock music, but the opportunity to play basketball? It's a ten-year window at best."

Kate suppressed her urge to giggle uncontrollably. Punk rock music? She'd been working out a riff from a Creedence Clearwater

Revival tune. That was so pre–punk rock, it was practically ancient.

"If it makes you feel any better, I don't see playing the guitar as my path in life," Kate had told her dad. "It's just something I do for fun."

Mr. Faber had taken a deep breath. "Sports are fun, Katie. If you want to have fun, play sports." Then he'd turned and walked down the hall.

Kate had waited a minute before closing her bedroom door, and she'd waited for a few more minutes after that before picking up her guitar again. When her dad had knocked on her door five minutes before, she'd been happy, and now she felt terrible. Kate felt guilty that she'd stopped going to the Y to play basketball with him, but it had started feeling sort of weird. The guys she and her dad played with had begun acting differently around her, like she might break or cry uncontrollably if they fouled her.

Kate stretched her arms toward her toes. It was funny how her mom seemed to get Kate's love of music and her dad didn't. Her dad was always going on about the importance of girls playing sports, but didn't he see that it was important for girls to play music, too? And not just pretty, I'm-so-sad-about-my-bad-boyfriend music, but music about being angry or excited, music about feeling crazy or weird or wild.

Now, sitting at the dinner table and listening to her dad talk about why man-to-man defenses were useless at the middle-school level of ball, Kate wondered if what she'd told her dad last fall was true. Had she really meant it when she'd said she didn't see playing guitar as her path in life? Well, she supposed the question was, a path to what? Kate wasn't thinking about becoming a famous rock-and-roll star or anything like that, though she could see putting out a CD on an independent label some day. But that wasn't really a path; that was just something she daydreamed about on the bus to school.

Here was the thing about guitar: When Kate played, she didn't worry about whether or not she was fat (she sort of thought she was, although Lorna insisted that Kate was perfectly normal), or when she was going to get her first period (her mom had been fifteen—*fifteen*!), or if she should try to fit in more and be like other girls. She didn't worry about grades. She didn't even worry about whether or not Matthew Holler was her boyfriend or a boy who was a friend who sometimes kissed her behind the garage. When Kate played guitar, she didn't worry about anything at all, except making the chords sound as clean or as soft or as fuzzy as she wanted them to sound.

Playing basketball had been like that too, she realized as she took a bite of baked potato. Maybe sports and music weren't so different. With basketball and guitar, you had to live precisely in the very moment you were living in. You had to train your mind not to wander off into the future or onto the topic of whether your zits were getting out of control.

"I'm thinking about trying out for the school musical," Kate said suddenly, surprising herself, and by the looks on their faces, the rest of her family too. "I think it's important to try new things. And besides, I like music."

Mr. Faber nodded, looking pleased. "I think that's great, Katie. Being in a musical is like being on a team, in a way. It's about working together, cooperating."

"Oh, Mel." Kate's mother sighed. "Being in a musical is about singing and self-expression. Enough with the sports analogies, honey."

"Being in a musical is about hanging out with geeks," Tracie offered through a mouthful of baked chicken. "The geekiest of the geeks. Computer nerds used to be the geekiest of the geeks, but now you never know if they might grow up to be billionaires. So now it's the musical kids who wear the geek crown."

"Good," Kate told her sister. "I like geeks."

"Enough," Mr. Faber told his daughters. He turned to Kate. "I think it's good you want to be involved. To be on a team."

Kate just nodded her head and gave her dad a big smile, like she thought he was absolutely right. Maybe he was. Kate didn't know. All she knew was she was tired of her dad looking at her like he wasn't quite sure who she was anymore.

. . .

"So did you hear?" Lorna asked when Kate met her in the auditorium ten minutes before auditions started on Friday afternoon. "The musical is going to be *Guys and Dolls*. It's about gangsters."

"Like *The Sopranos*?" Kate asked, sitting down. "Isn't that sort of bloody for middle school?"

"No, it's about *funny* gangsters," Lorna informed her. "Like from the 1930s or something. I don't know anything about it besides that." She turned to Kate. "Give me your honest opinion—should I try out for the lead? I'm not that great of a singer, but I think it would make my mom happy."

Kate scanned the crowd of auditioners. "Well, I see Phoebe Washington, who has a great voice, and Ginny Woo, also great. The entire middle-school chorus is here . . . and . . . whoa!"

"Whoa what?" Lorna asked anxiously. "Somebody even better than Phoebe?"

Kate shook her head. "Flannery's here."

Flannery was sitting by herself in the back of the auditorium, and if Kate was seeing things clearly, she was knitting. What was Flannery doing at tryouts? And since when had she been a knitter? This was all too weird.

"Is her hair still pink?" Lorna asked, straining to see where Flannery was sitting.

"It's red now," Kate informed her. "She's talking about doing purplc ncxt."

"Well, go find out what she's doing here," Lorna said, practically pushing Kate out of her seat. "I'm dying to know."

Lorna found Flannery fascinating. It was like Flannery did the things Lorna dreamed of doing but really didn't want to do—like dye her hair purple. Lorna wasn't really a purple-hair person, but she liked the idea of being a purple-hair person, and so she liked the idea of Flannery, even though when Kate offered to introduce her, Lorna had said no thanks. Flannery was a little too nervous-making, in Lorna's opinion.

Kate thought Lorna and Flannery would hit it off, but she didn't try to force them together. The fact was, Flannery *was* pretty cranky. Kate was used to Flannery's crankiness, but Lorna might take it the wrong way.

Sure enough, Flannery's expression was pure grouch when Kate reached her row. "I keep dropping stitches," she complained, holding up a knitting needle for Kate to see. "It's driving me crazy."

"I didn't know you even knew how to knit," Kate said, sitting down. "Are you just learning how?"

Flannery nodded. "I've been reading all this DIY stuff online—you know, grow your own food, make your own clothes. Megan got me into it. I'm trying to make a sweater, but I royally suck at it."

"My mom knits, if you need any advice," Kate told her. "Mostly she knits socks and gives them away."

"I totally want to learn how to knit socks," Flannery said, looping a strand of yarn around a needle. "I want to be able to make all my own clothes, underwear included."

"That's cool," Kate said. Onstage, some teachers had started to gather—Mr. Periello, the chorus director, and the drama teacher, Ms. South—and people had started to whisper, like things were about to get started. "So, are you trying out for the play?"

"No, I'm here to conduct a scientific study," Flannery replied. "What do you think?"

Kate couldn't tell whether Flannery was being sarcastic or not. Flannery was the sort of person who pretty much always sounded sarcastic or annoyed. "I think it would be hard to conduct a scientific experiment while you're knitting."

Flannery raised her eyebrows. "You'd be surprised what you can do with a pair of knitting needles."

"Probably," Kate said. "But really—are you auditioning or not?"

"Of course I'm auditioning. Why else would I be here?"

"To conduct a scientific experiment?"

Flannery laughed. "I'm taking drama for my elective, and Ms. South is giving extra credit to everyone who auditions. I can act, but I can't sing, so there's no way I'll actually get a part. But I'll get extra credit."

It always surprised Kate that Flannery

cared about her grades. Flannery seemed like the sort of person who wouldn't care if she flunked out. But at the end of every quarter, when the honor roll was posted outside of the front office, Flannery's name was always on it, no matter what color her hair was or how bad her attitude had been the last three months.

"By the way, it's still big news about the Matthew-Emily split," Flannery said, squinting at her knitting like she'd lost something inside of it. "Emily's telling everyone it's your fault."

"That's dumb," Kate said, staring straight ahead. She didn't know if this was something she wanted to discuss with Flannery. Flannery hung out with the same group of eighth graders as Matthew did, the ones with vaguely bad attitudes and lots of black T-shirts, so she'd know what was really going on. But sometimes Flannery was a little too honest for Kate's comfort level. Sometimes Kate could live without Flannery's opinion.

"Yeah, that's what Matthew says too," Flannery said. "He says you guys are just friends. He broke up with Emily because he wanted to be free."

"He did?" Kate felt her stomach fill with butterflies, the bad kind, the kind with poison on their little proboscises. "He does? Want to be free, I mean?"

"Sure," Flannery replied, poking her right-hand needle into a left-hand needle loop. "Everybody was totally amazed when he got together with Emily in the first place. Although now he says she was never really his girlfriend. But if she wasn't, then why did he have to break up with her?"

"Yeah, that's a good point," Kate said, her voice sounding hollow. "Well, it looks like things are about to get started." She stood up, amazed by how much she felt like a zombie, someone who had been dead for a while now but had miraculously retained the ability to walk and talk.

"Hey, Kate," Flannery said, and Kate turned around. She was surprised by Flannery's sympathetic expression. "You know that the Matthew Hollers of the world always make better friends than boyfriends, right?"

Kate nodded, though she wasn't sure she

knew that at all. "I need to go try out now," she said in a flat voice.

The walk back to the front row took Kate approximately five hundred years. Maybe it was because her legs had turned into rubber. Maybe it was because time had slowed down until every clock in the world barely budged. Maybe, she thought, it was because when you realize that you're nothing, nobody, nada, just a silly girl who thought she might be someone somebody else could fall in love with, then it occurs to you that there's no reason to get any place anytime soon.

When she finally reached her seat, Lorna leaned over and said, "What's wrong? Your face is totally white. You look like a ghost."

"I am a ghost," Kate told her, and then Mr. Periello called her name, so she stood back up and walked to the stage, where she sang an old Joni Mitchell song her mom liked a lot called "Both Sides Now." When she finished, everybody in the audience clapped and stomped their feet, and a few people whistled. Mr. Periello looked at her a long time before saying, "That was beautiful, Kate. I had no idea you could sing like that."

The funny thing was, Kate couldn't really sing like that. Or at least she'd never sung like that before. But then again, she'd never had a broken heart before. Maybe that's what had to happen to you before you could really sing, before your song was more than just a collection of notes and words that came out of your mouth.

When Kate got back to her seat, Flannery was sitting in it. Kate sat down beside her and stared straight ahead. When Lorna leaned toward Kate to say something, Kate held up her hand and said, "I can't talk right now."

Flannery worked a few stitches of her sweater, which was beginning to resemble a piece of Swiss cheese. Then she laid her knitting on her lap and, without looking directly at Kate, said, "If I had to guess, I would say he really does like you. The problem is, it doesn't matter."

Kate nodded. She thought about kissing Matthew Holler behind her garage. She knew he'd really meant it, even if he didn't act like it now. She wondered how a person could do that, feel one way and act another. Kate couldn't. Her dad said she had no poker face, and it was true. If she was mad, she growled, and if she was happy, she laughed. Maybe she just didn't have any interest in faking her life, or maybe she was just too stupid to figure out how to pretend like she didn't care.

Although, hadn't she been pretending the last two weeks like she didn't care?

The kiss behind the garage. They'd been writing songs together at Matthew's house, and when Kate said she had to go home, Matthew offered to walk her. A light snow had started falling when they were halfway to Kate's house, and Matthew had launched into a loud rendition of "Let it Snow."

"That's a Christmas carol," Kate had admonished him. "You can't sing Christmas carols in January!"

"What does 'Let it Snow' have to do with Christmas?" Matthew had asked. "It's totally about the weather. It's a weather song, like 'Singin' in the Rain' or 'Blowin' in the Wind.'"

Kate had cracked up. "'Blowin' in the Wind' isn't a weather song. It's a protest song."

Matthew had slung his arm around Kate's shoulder. "That's what I like about you, Faber. I don't know any other girl who would know that."

"Lots of girls know that," Kate had insisted, although she was secretly proud that among all the girls she personally knew, she was the only one who had a clue to what "Blowin' in the Wind" was about. "Girls are as into music as guys are. At least some girls. And not all guys are into music. My dad is a total music dork. His big claim to fame is that he saw Bon Jovi three times when he was in college. But you know what's cool? My mom saw the Clash. Twice."

"Not to one-up you or anything, but my mom toured with the Clash."

Kate had stopped in her tracks. "No way!"

"Well, maybe that's an exaggeration. But she was friends with some sound guy's girlfriend, and so when the Clash toured the Eastern Seaboard, my mom went with them for a few shows."

"Maybe my mom should invite your mom over for coffee," Kate had said, immediately liking the idea of her family and Matthew's getting tangled up, making it harder for Matthew to untangle himself from Kate. Of course, if their moms got to be friends, and the Hollers started to feel like family, then Kate and Matthew might start feeling like cousins, which wasn't the vibe Kate was going for.

I'm such an idiot for thinking like this, she had told herself, sticking out her tongue to catch a snowflake. I mean, get a life.

They'd reached Kate's house by then. The sky had gotten dark, and there had been a layer of intensely pink clouds on the horizon. Kate had pointed at it and said, "I'm normally not a pink person, but I think that's beautiful."

Matthew hadn't said anything, and for a second Kate had felt really stupid, but she'd stopped feeling stupid when he'd grabbed her hand and pulled her to the side of the Fabers' garage. Instead of feeling stupid, she'd felt jittery and light-headed, and when Matthew had pulled her toward him and dipped his face toward hers, she'd thought she might possibly faint.

Matthew had brushed a strand of hair away from Kate's face and said, "You are totally awesome. You are really, totally awesome."

And then he'd kissed her, and his lips had been so soft Kate could hardly stand it. She'd put her hand in his hair, the way she'd wanted to ever since she first saw him, tangling her fingers in his reddish-gold curls.

She'd thought it meant something. She'd really thought it meant something, and so she'd tried not to care when he didn't call the next day, and then on Tuesday back at school when he didn't act like anything special had happened between them, she tried even harder not to care. And so maybe it wasn't surprising that all her not caring (which was really caring more than anything in the world) had poured out in the song she'd just sung.

She just couldn't hold it in anymore.

On Monday, the cast list was posted. Kate and Lorna were both in the chorus. Lorna was incensed. "You should have gotten the lead!" she told Kate at lunch. "You were awesome."

Kate had gotten at least ten phone calls over the weekend, some from people she hardly knew, telling her how awesome her singing had been. She'd felt weirdly famous for forty-eight hours.

Now she turned to Lorna and said, "I'm really tired of the word 'awesome.' It doesn't really mean anything. It's like a blank word that people use when they can't think of something real to say."

Lorna frowned. "I'd be offended, except I can tell you're in a bad mood about something, which probably has to do with Matthew Holler, who is totally *not* awesome, in my opinion. Which is something I think you need to tell him."

"What are you talking about?" Kate stared at Lorna. "He hasn't done anything."

"Exactly my point," Lorna said, chewing on a piece of biscotti. "He kissed you, and then—nothing."

"It's not like he stopped talking to me," Kate pointed out.

"Really, Kate? *Really?* That's really going to be your standard of acceptable behavior when it comes to guys?"

Kate shrugged. Maybe. Well, not all guys, but at least when it came to Matthew Holler. She would put up with anything—

And then she stopped. If Marylin had been saying these things to Kate about Benjamin, Kate would have been furious. She would have been telling Marylin to have some self-respect. She, Kate, would have marched right up to Benjamin and yelled at him about how he treated girls and other living creatures, and she might have even kicked him in the shins, although in general Kate preferred to be the nonviolent type.

Kate took a deep breath. She wrapped up her sandwich and put it back in her backpack. "Excuse me," she said, "but I need to go have a talk with someone."

"You bet you do," Lorna agreed.

But when Kate got to the audio lab, she didn't know what to say. Matthew was sitting in his usual seat, working on a track for a project he was calling *World of Noise*. He didn't turn around when Kate walked in, and she thought maybe she wouldn't say anything at all, maybe she would just throw a pencil at his back and walk out.

Finally she cleared her throat and mumbled, "Hey, Matthew."

He turned around. "Hey, Kate! You've got to listen to the edits I've done. Totally awesome."

And that was what pushed Kate over the edge. Completely, entirely, all the way over the edge.

"You will never be a songwriter if you can't come up with a better adjective than 'awesome' to describe things," she said, and she could feel the tips of her ears turning red, she was so mad. "Songwriters are supposed to find the exact right words. Precise words. Definite words. So quit calling everything 'awesome,' and quit calling me 'awesome' if you don't mean it."

"But I do mean it," Matthew said, sounding confused. "You're the most awesome girl I know."

Kate stomped across the room and stood

two feet in front of Matthew. She pointed her finger at him. "I am not awesome. I am not any adjective you can think of, since you couldn't think of a decent adjective to save your life. You know why you say I'm totally awesome? Because you don't have the guts to say any-thing real."

She decided that was all that she had to say. What else was there? You kissed me behind the garage, but now you act like you didn't, and that makes me mad? Stupid. It wasn't some-thing they could have a debate over.

But it was interesting, Kate had to admit, that Matthew's face had gone all red, like he was coming down with a sudden case of the flu. Didn't that mean he at least cared a little bit? His lips seemed to be twitching, like there were words inside his mouth that he was trying very hard not to let out.

But finally the words escaped. "I can't marry you, okay?" Matthew said, pounding his fists on his knees. "I'm sorry, but that's just how it is."

Kate's eyes widened. Her mouth dropped open as though her jaw had suddenly become unhinged. "What? What did you just say? Do you think I want to *marry* you? That's crazy. I'm in seventh grade. You know that, right?"

Matthew waved his hands in front of his face, like he was trying to make what he'd just said disappear. "No! That's not what I'm saying. What I mean is—man, I don't know what I mean. It made more sense in my head. Like, you're my best friend, okay? And if we were thirty or something, we'd probably get married and play guitar every night after dinner, and it would be totally awesome. But we're not thirty, and I don't know what to do about you."

Kate just stood there. She'd always thought that the first time a boy told her he loved her, it would be all romantic, all starlight and birds singing, a voice whispering in her ear. She hadn't thought the soundtrack would be *World of Noise*.

"Well, quit kissing me, okay?" she said. "Because I can't deal with you kissing me and then acting like I don't matter to you."

Matthew threw his head back and laughed, sounding relieved. "Dude, you're the *only* person who matters. Get a grip."

Suddenly the door to the audio lab opened, and Kate turned to find herself face-to-face with Flannery.

"I thought you'd be here," Flannery said. "You're not going to believe this, but I made the cut."

"You did?" Kate was confused. "I didn't see your name on the cast list."

"Yeah, well, Audrey Fischer just got suspended for skipping class for the third time this quarter, so I got bumped up. I guess I'm headed for Broadway." Flannery peered over Kate's shoulder. "Hey, Matthew, you're an idiot," she called out, and then grabbed Kate's hand. "Come with me to get my script. I don't think I have any lines, but I should check, just in case."

Kate didn't really want to leave. She wanted to spend the rest of the period listening to Matthew tell her she was the only person who mattered to him, even if they wouldn't be kissing each other anymore. Maybe they could kiss each other again later. Maybe when they were sixteen. She thought it might be nice to spend some more time talking about how great

Matthew thought she was, but she guessed there'd be time for that later. So she followed Flannery out into the hallway.

"Do you really think Matthew's an idiot?" she asked, interested in Flannery's opinion. If you'd asked Kate an hour ago whether she thought Matthew Holler was an idiot, she would definitely have said yes, but now she didn't think so. Now she thought he was possibly extremely brilliant.

Flannery laughed. "Only in the ways that matter."

They passed by the gym. Inside, a few of the girls from the basketball team were practicing free throws. Kate thought about going in and joining them, just to get that feeling you had after you sent the ball through the hoop without touching the rim. It was like you had control over gravity. It was like you could make anything happen that you felt like.

Flannery grabbed her arm. "Come on, slowpoke, let's go sing really loud and be stars."

Kate nodded. Singing would be good too. Maybe next year she'd do both, sing and play basketball. Not at the same time, of course, although thinking about it made her laugh. She wondered what her dad would think if she became the singing point guard. The rock-and-roll rebounder.

I don't know if that's the right path for you, Katie, her dad would probably say. But Kate didn't care. She was pretty sure the right path was the path she was on this very second, walking down the hall with Flannery, in this totally awesome world.

When Marylin got to cheerleading practice on Friday afternoon, she was surprised to see Benjamin Huddle sitting on the bleachers, waiting for her. It was a "What's Wrong with This Picture?" moment, where you had to look around for what didn't fit in. Benjamin Huddle definitely didn't fit into cheerleading practice. He wasn't an athlete, for one thing. Sometimes a bunch of football or basketball players would stand around and watch the first few minutes of practice before the cheerleading coach, Ms. Wells, shooed them away, and that didn't seem strange. After all, if it weren't for the athletes, why were the cheerleaders practicing in the first place? Who would they cheer for?

Not for the Student Government leaders, that was for sure, though thinking about it, Marylin could see how that would be a nice thing. After all, athletes didn't actually contribute all that much to the school, but the Student Government leaders got stuff for students, like extra parties and more pizza days in the cafeteria. Didn't that deserve a cheer or two?

But that wasn't how things worked, and so it was strange to see Benjamin Huddle in a world where he didn't quite belong. But the strangeness of the situation didn't keep Marylin from feeling as though she'd just been injected with helium. Every part of her suddenly felt lighter and slightly tingly. When Benjamin caught sight of her and broke into a huge grin, Marylin wanted to snuggle in beside him on the bleachers and inhale the wonderful smell of him, which mostly came from the fabric softener his mom used on their laundry (Downy, which Marylin knew because she'd asked Benjamin the other day and then made her mom go buy some right away).

"What are you doing here?" Marylin asked, trying to keep the giddiness out of her voice in case any of the other cheerleaders were close enough to hear. "I thought you had to go help your mom with her art class."

"I do," Benjamin told her. "She's going to pick me up in ten minutes. So I thought I'd come watch your practice until it was time to meet her."

"Really?" Marilyn asked, amazed. "You don't think that would be boring?"

Benjamin grinned. "It's only ten minutes."

Marilyn couldn't think of anything else to say, so she just stood there, smiling. She'd never liked a boy this way before, not in a real kind of way that was more than a crush, so she hadn't had any way of knowing beforehand how much time she would spend with a big, dumb smile plastered across her face. Of course, as a middle-school cheerleader, she did a lot of automatic smiling, but it wasn't the sort of smiling where her whole face played a part in it. It was strictly lip smiling when she walked down the hall in official cheerleader capacity.

"I also wanted to run an idea by you," Benjamin said. "I just had a meeting with Mrs. Calhoun about Student Government stuff, and she said we actually have extra money in the budget this year to fund a new project, or to give more money to an extracurricular activity, or whatever. I was thinking we should have some sort of contest. You know, let the students decide how we should use the money. I mean, it *is* kind of their money, if you think about it. It comes from their parents' taxes."

"We could use new cheerleading uniforms," Marylin said, smiling her best enthusiastic Student Government representative smile. "The ones we have now are getting shabby. It's bad for school spirit when the cheerleaders look sloppy."

"Sure," Benjamin said, not sounding all that convinced. "That could be one of the suggestions students vote on."

"Or we could just not vote, and give the

cheerleaders the money," Marylin said in a sing-songy, I'm-sort-of-joking-but-sort-of-not voice.

Benjamin shook his head and laughed. "We could. That would make it easier, for sure. But I don't know. I think it's better if everybody gets to make suggestions."

Marylin shrugged. "Maybe. But think about my idea, okay? Because it's really important to me. And it would make me happy."

Benjamin reddened and looked down at his shoes. "Okay. Yeah, sure."

"Let's get going, Marylin!" Coach Wells called over, and Marylin gave Benjamin an apologetic look.

"I don't think Coach is going to let you watch practice," she warned him. "At least not for long. She's pretty strict about keeping prac-tices closed."

"I've got to go anyway." Benjamin stood up. "My mom's probably waiting out front. She's always early. I'll call you, okay?"

"Okay," Marylin said. She watched as he climbed down the bleachers, then called out, "Bye! Call me!"

A tiny seed of worry planted itself in her brain. Was Benjamin mad at her? Hurrying over to the other side of the gym, where everyone was warming up, Marylin tried to shake the idea out of her head. Why would he be mad at her? All she did was make a suggestion.

"What were you talking to Benjamin about?" Mazie asked her as she pulled a knee to her chest. "You looked idiotically cheerful over there."

"Nothing," Marylin said, running a hand through her hair, trying to sound casual. "He was just telling me there's some extra Student Government money, and I was saying that we should definitely use it to get new uniforms."

Mazie bent over at the waist and reached for her toes. "You're sure it's not because you were talking to Benjie-wenjie? Take my advice, Marylin, and don't become emotionally attached to Geek Boy over there. Believe me, he's not your type."

Marylin tried to smile in a way that suggested this wasn't a problem at all. "Don't worry about me. I know exactly what I'm doing."

"Are you sure?" Mazie reached back to grab

her foot in a hamstring stretch. "Because you looked a little too happy over there, talking to him. Like maybe you're interested in something besides new uniforms."

Marylin suddenly had a crazy impulse to tell the truth. *I am in love with Benjamin Huddle,* she wanted to declare. *He's nice and funny and smart and cute. If you had any sense, you'd be in love with him too.*

But Mazie was staring at her with that steely-eyed look that made Marylin feel like she was a five-year-old in a room full of sophisticated teenagers. So instead of declaring her love for Benjamin, she just said, "I don't get why you care so much. It's sort of weird."

Which was maybe the wrong thing to say.

Mazie put her hands on her hips and leaned toward Marylin. "Are you saying you *do* like Benjamin Huddle?" she hissed. "Because that's a problem that I definitely care about. It's my *job* to care about it."

"Your job?"

"Yes, my job." Mazie took a step back and sighed deeply. "You're so dumb sometimes, I can hardly stand it. Look around you," she said, waving her arm at the cheerleaders in various stages of warming up. "We all have jobs. Your job is to be pretty. My job is to make sure you don't mess up and have a geeky boyfriend."

Marylin stood very still. She felt like she was standing on a very narrow ledge and could fall off if the breeze shifted the slightest bit. The weird thing was, she could feel herself sort of wanting to fall. "Well," she started slowly, "I guess what I don't know is, who hired you? I mean, how did you get this job?"

Mazie stared at her. "Watch out, Marylin. You're about to get in very serious trouble."

Ruby Santiago sauntered over to where they were standing. "What's going on?" she asked, smiling even though she sounded worried. "You guys seem kind of stressed out."

This is the time to act like everything's fine, Marylin told herself. This is the time to pull yourself together. "I was just telling Mazie there's money in the school budget for new uniforms. That's what I was talking with Benjamin Huddle about."

Ruby's face brightened. "I am *so* sick of the uniforms we have now, aren't you? They're totally fourth grade."

Marylin nodded. "Exactly. That's what I've been saying all year. We should start getting input from everybody about what they want the new uniforms to look like."

"Ruby's captain," Mazie said, inserting herself between Ruby and Marylin. "She should decide."

"Well, me and Coach Wells," Ruby said agreeably. "But if other people have ideas, I'd love to hear them." She patted Marylin on the shoulder. "Nice work."

Marylin shrugged and smiled modestly. "Anything for the squad, right, Mazie?"

Mazie harrumphed, but left it at that.

Marylin trotted over to where several of the cheerleaders were stretched out on the floor and sat down next to Caitlin Moore. "How's your knee?" she asked Caitlin, whose knee had been hurting for several days now. "Any better?"

Caitlin glanced over at Ruby, who smiled and waved, and then turned and smiled at

Marylin. "I've been icing it a lot, just like Coach said to. It's definitely less sore."

"That's awesome!" Marylin said, feeling pretty awesome herself. Things with the other cheerleaders had been feeling strained, but now she felt like she was in again. Ruby was more powerful than Mazie, and if Marylin got new cheerleading uniforms, she could probably be Ruby's second in command. Normally Marylin wasn't someone who was all that interested in power, but she was starting to see how it could come in handy.

She stretched out her legs and leaned over them, reaching for her toes. Marylin imagined the squad in cute new uniforms, the skirts slightly shorter than the ones they had now, the tops barely skimming their belly buttons. She imagined Benjamin gazing adoringly at her from the stands, and her parents waving from where they sat at every basketball game, two rows behind the home bench, Petey in between them, cheering the cheerleaders. That was Marylin's favorite part of every game— seeing her family looking like a family again.

All she had to do was get those new uniforms. Then everything else in her life would fall into place.

Marylin was surprised to find Kate riding home on the activity bus that afternoon. Kate wasn't an activities person, for the most part. She was the sort of person who liked to get home as soon as school was over.

"What did you stay after for?" Marylin asked Kate, sitting down beside her. "Did you have Creative Writing Club today?"

"That's on Tuesdays," Kate said. "I had play rehearsal today, only we weren't doing any of my scenes, and so I helped Matthew in the audio lab. He's doing this whole *World of Noise* project for extra credit in science. It's really cool."

"Is it all noisy and screechy?" Marylin asked, shuddering a little, imagining the sort of noises she hated, like Styrofoam cups being torn apart and microphone feedback.

Kate nodded. "Pretty much. It's better not to listen to it with the volume up too high."

"So are you and Matthew still hanging out a lot?" Marylin asked, hoping to get the conversation on a more interesting track. "I mean, are you a thing?"

"No, we're not a *thing*," Kate said, sounding sort of defensive about it. "We're friends. We have a lot in common."

"But you wish you were a thing, right?" Marylin prodded. She knew she was making Kate mad, but sometimes Kate's don't-make-such-a-big-deal-about-everything attitude got on her nerves. Since when was it against the law to ask your friends if they liked somebody?

"I don't wish anything." Kate frowned and looked out the window. "Not everything is about hearts and romance, Marylin. It's okay just to be friends with people."

Marylin nodded. "Definitely. But it's okay to be in love with them too. Even if you're just friends. I mean, no one's going to arrest you if you say you've got a crush on somebody."

"Maybe they should," Kate muttered, but now she didn't sound so mad. "Maybe it would be a good idea if people talked about something else for a change. I mean, we're in seventh grade. It's not like we're going to meet the person we're going to marry. So why not just hang out with other people instead of having to put a label on everything?"

Marylin shrugged. "Sure, if that's what you want to do. But I think it's okay to like a guy even if you're not going to marry him. It's like practicing for when the guy you're going to marry comes along. And you never know— maybe Benjamin and I will get married some-day." Marylin paused. That thought was a little scary even to her. "I mean, after we've dated other people and gone to college and all that."

"I guess practicing at love is good," Kate said, sounding like she halfway believed it. "I get that. But being friends is good too. Living your life is good."

"Right," Marylin agreed. "We can agree. Both ways are good."

Marylin leaned back in her seat, feeling pleased that for once in their lives she and Kate had come to a compromise. She especially appreciated it after the past few months of being bossed around by Mazie and the other cheerleaders. She'd almost forgotten what having a real friend was like.

And then inspiration hit her. "I've got a great idea! Why don't you spend the night at my house tonight? We can watch movies and eat a ton of pizza. And we could even do a makeover. Not that you need a makeover! I didn't mean it like that. But I could show you how to put on just a touch of eyeliner, maybe a little bit of blush. And maybe you could borrow some of my clothes?"

The idea of giving Kate a makeover made Marylin happy. Maybe she was on Mazie's bad side, but she could still do some good in the world.

"I like my clothes," Kate said, sounding stubborn. "Besides, all the eyeliner in the world won't make me beautiful. Which I don't even care about, by the way."

Marylin wagged a finger. "But it would turn you into a prettier Kate. And I know you're like this poet and everything, but that doesn't mean you can't be pretty, too, right? Because you *are* pretty, Kate."

"Really?" Kate looked at Marylin as though she desperately wanted to believe her. "Do you really think so?"

Marylin nodded. "I know so. So what do you say? Sleepover?"

"Okay," Kate said, sounding a little reluctant. "I guess."

Excellent! At last Marylin was going to give Kate the makeover she'd been dying to give her for years. "Listen, after I get through with you, you can have your pick of guys. Just you wait."

"You know, it's possible you need professional help," Kate said, hugging her arms to her chest. "I mean, you're starting to scare me."

"Good," Marylin said, laughing. "Be afraid. Be very afraid."

How long had it been since Kate had spent the night at her house? Marylin wondered as she made up the second bed in her bedroom later that afternoon. Well, there was the sleepover last summer, but Kate had spent the whole time watching TV with Petey. They'd had a sleepover once in sixth grade, with Brittany and Kyla and Emma. That seemed like ten thousand years ago. Marylin had still been friends with Flannery then, which was almost impossible to believe. How had that happened? One day, she'd been best friends with Kate, the next day Flannery had moved in across the street and taken over Marylin's life.

"Kate's such a baby," Flannery had said a week or so after meeting Marylin. "I don't know how you can be friends with her."

The thing was, Marylin had sort of been thinking the same thing. Kate seemed like a little kid, and Marylin was ready to grow up. She was ready for makeup and group dates and *Seventeen* magazine. Kate was ready to spend all weekend watching the *Mythbusters* marathon and making rubber-band balls. Marylin was starting to feel like she'd sort of outgrown Kate. So when Flannery came along, a year older, a year more sophisticated, a room stocked with *Seventeen*s and *Teen Vogue*s and every color of nail polish imaginable, well, it had seemed like fate to Marylin. Flannery was clearly the next step for her to take.

Now she felt bad for the times she and Flannery had given Kate the silent treatment; in fact, Marylin liked to skip right over that part of her life. She hoped Kate wouldn't bring it up tonight. Although Marylin did sort of want to ask Kate about Flannery, since the two of them had become friends. Not best friends— these days Kate seemed to be best friends with that girl Lorna—but definitely friends. How had that happened?

Seventh grade was so different, Marylin thought as she slipped Kate's pillow into a pillow-case. Everyone just seemed to go their own way. Marylin had started it, she supposed, by becoming a cheerleader last spring, but look at Kate. How many years had she eaten at the same lunch table with Marcie Grossman and Brittany Lamb and Amber Colbaugh? And suddenly, just like that, last October she and Lorna had become lunch buddies, sitting by themselves at a small table near the exit, laughing and chatting away.

Flannery hung out with the eighth-grade delinquents, of course. Come to think of it, Marylin had seen Kate sitting with them earlier in the week. She really hoped Kate wasn't going to start taking drugs. Kate wouldn't do that, would she? She wasn't that kind of person. Sure, she was independent and maybe a little rebellious, but you could be those things without living a life of crime, couldn't you?

Marylin suddenly wondered if inviting Kate to spend the night had been such a good idea. What if Kate had cigarettes and wanted to smoke them in Marylin's bathroom? She *so* did not want to go there with Kate. They'd known each other since preschool. It would be too weird if Kate wanted to smoke. It would be like the girl Marylin had known all her life was gone, replaced by a stranger.

I miss Rhetta, Marylin thought, falling back on her bed and staring at the ceiling. But she didn't just miss Rhetta, she realized; she missed Rhetta's family. Sure, Rhetta's parents were strict, but they were also nice and funny and *there*. Right now Rhetta was bowling with her family and other families from her church. Marylin wondered if she could get her parents to start going to Rhetta's church. They wouldn't have to sit together, but maybe on bowling nights, Marylin's dad could come over and pick up Marylin, her mom, and Petey, and they could be a family together that way. And Marylin wouldn't have to worry about anyone smoking, because people didn't smoke when they were doing church stuff.

"Marylin, Kate's here!" Petey called from downstairs. "I'm going to show her my gecko!"

Please don't want to smoke cigarettes, Marylin thought, standing up and checking her hair in the mirror. Please just be Kate.

She found Kate in the kitchen, where she was getting a lecture on the care and feeding of lizards.

"Pretty fascinating, huh?" Marylin asked, rolling her eyes.

Kate shrugged. "It is, sort of. I mean, reptiles aren't exactly my thing, but I get why Petey's into them."

Petey beamed. Marylin was pretty sure he

had a secret crush on Kate. Probably because Kate was the only one of Marylin's friends who acknowledged his existence.

"Let's go upstairs," Marylin said. "My mom's going to order pizza in a little while."

When they got to Marylin's room, Kate put her bag down on the bed and started looking around. "It's different in here," she said. "You took down your Hello Kitty posters. Didn't you used to say you would always love Hello Kitty, even when you were fifty?"

"Did I say that?" Marylin didn't remember ever saying that, but she supposed she could have, especially around fourth grade, when she was Hello Kitty obsessed. "Well, I'm thirteen now, and I'm pretty much over Hello Kitty already. But who knows? Maybe when I'm fifty, I'll get really into it again."

"Or maybe when you're eighty, right before you die," Kate said, sitting down at Marylin's desk. "The circle of life and all that stuff." She picked up Marylin's ballerina snow globe. "I remember this! Gracie McRae gave it to you in second grade, right before she moved."

"Because we took ballet gather," Marylin said, nodding. "Only she was really horrible. She just sort of clomped all over the place. But it was nice of her to give me the snow globe."

"It's weird how well I can remember her," Kate said, shaking the globe and watching the little flakes fall on the ballerina's head. "She and George Kenley had the same birthday, and George's mom brought cupcakes with M&Ms on them, and Gracie's mom brought banana muffins, and everybody wanted the M&M cupcakes. Do you remember that?"

Marylin shook her head. "No, not really. But I remember that she always smelled like peanut butter."

"See, I don't remember that at all."

Marylin plopped down on her bed and faced Kate. "I wish they'd given out yearbooks in elementary school, so we could compare everybody back then to how they are now. Like, I remember Laurie Wochek from kindergarten, and she wasn't even the least bit cute. She was round and pudgy with two million freckles. But now she's really pretty. It's like it happened overnight."

"I think it's weird to see Franklin Boyd with zits," Kate said. "It's not like they're that bad, but they just look weird on him. I've known him since preschool—what's he doing with zits?"

"He's always had a baby face," Marylin agreed. "Zits seem entirely out of place."

They lapsed into silence. Was this what it meant to have a history with someone? Marylin wondered. To be able to remember all the same things from preschool and second grade? Maybe. She liked how it made her feel comfortable with Kate, sort of like they were family.

Almost as if she'd read Marylin's mind, Kate said, "It's weird to be here without your dad in the house. Because if your dad was here, by now he would have popped his head in the room and said something silly. You know, 'We're having barbecued beet loaf for dinner—hope you brought your appetite!'"

"Yeah," Marylin said, her voice catching a little bit in her throat. "He liked to clown around when you were here. When he was growing up, his mom had bad migraines all the time, and he couldn't ever have friends come over. So it made him happy when our friends were in the house. We don't know anyone where he lives now, so that's not going to happen anymore, I guess."

"Do you think—?" Kate started, then stopped herself.

"What?"

"Well, that your parents might get back together? Because they did hang out on Christmas Eve, right? So maybe they're thinking about it?"

Marylin looked at her feet. "I don't think so. The weird thing is they sort of get along better now than before they were divorced. They sit at all the home games together to watch me cheer, and the other night they were talking on the phone and my mom was laughing her head off. After she hung up, she said, 'Your dad cracks me up,' and then she sort of looked like she wished she hadn't said it, like she didn't want us to get the wrong idea."

"Maybe they're starting to like each other again," Kate suggested. "Who knows what might happen?"

Marylin nodded, swallowing hard. "I just don't want to get my hopes up."

The phone rang two seconds later, and Marylin wondered if it might be Benjamin. Maybe he'd thought over her cheerleading uniform idea and decided he liked it. "I better get this," she said, reaching over to pick her phone up off the desk.

"It might be Benjamin," Kate said, echoing Marylin's thoughts again. "Maybe he's going to ask you to the prom."

"Like we even have a middle-school prom," Marylin complained. "All we have is the stupid spring dance. They have a real prom at Githens, did you know that?"

"The news media had not alerted me to that fact," Kate replied dryly. "I'll go write my congressperson immediately."

Marylin ignored Kate's sarcasm and looked at the phone's screen. "It's Mazie," she reported. "I guess I should talk to her. She's not very happy with me right now."

And just like that, the feeling between Marylin and Kate changed. Marylin could feel it. The friendly vibe that had filled the room disappeared.

"I dare you not to answer," Kate said. "I dare you to say *no* to Mazie Calloway for once in your life."

"You don't understand," Marylin said. "That's not how my life works." She held the phone up to her ear. "Hey, Mazie!" she said in her best, cheerful middle-school cheerleader voice, a huge smile plastered across her face for good measure. "What's up?"

"Me and Ruby are about to go to the mall and get mani-pedis," Mazie announced. "You're coming with us. Ruby's noticed that you don't really seem to be keeping up your appearance lately. You're getting sloppy."

Marylin was taken aback. She'd just done her nails two days ago! "Maybe I had a bad day on Wednesday," she said, trying to placate Mazie. "But I did my nails that night, and I've worn preplanned outfits every day this week. I don't think that's sloppy at all."

"Ruby thinks you should come," Mazie said. "She *is* captain of the squad."

"Well, I can't," Marylin said, doing her best to sound sorry about it. "I've got—stuff."

"Are you going over to your dad's tonight?"

"Um, yes, uh-huh," Marylin said. She was suddenly very conscious that Kate was listening to the conversation. "That's right."

"So why did you tell Ashley to pick you up at your mom's house in the morning?" Mazie replied in a *gotcha!* tone of voice.

Marylin scrambled for an answer. "My dad's bringing me back later."

Kate leaned toward her and whispered, "Do you want me to talk to her?"

"Who's that?" Mazie sounded scandalized. "Is that Kate Faber? What is she doing there?"

Marylin panicked and said the stupidest thing in the world. "She's just dropping something off."

Kate stood up. "That's right," she declared in a loud voice. "And I'm leaving now."

"Mazie, I've got to go," Marylin said, wildly waving at Kate to stay put. "I'll call you later."

"We'll be there in fifteen minutes," Mazie told her. "You better be ready."

Marylin could hear Kate stomping down the stairs in her big black boots.

"I really can't," she told Mazie. "I've got—"

"Yeah, I know, you've got stuff. Well, get unstuffed. I mean it, Marylin. You're crossing the line. You're totally out of control."

And with that, Mazie was gone.

The door slammed. Kate was gone too.

Marylin walked over to her desk and picked up the ballerina snow globe. This was it. This was when she had to make the decision. Mazie wasn't going to let her straddle both sides of the line forever—in fact, she wasn't going to let her straddle both sides of the line for ten more minutes. Even if Marylin delivered new uniforms to the squad every season, even if she got on Ruby's good side and became the second most powerful girl in the school, Marylin was going to have to choose, cheerleading and popularity versus everything else—Benjamin Huddle, Rhetta, Kate, Student Government.

Marylin turned the globe over and shook it up. Gracie McRae. She'd been the worst ballet dancer in the world! Marylin wondered what she was like now. Had she gotten pretty? Was she still nice? Was she a cheerleader? A jock? No, probably not a jock. You had to be a lot more coordinated than Gracie McRae to be a jock. Maybe she was one of those girls who spent their Friday nights baking cookies for the homeless shelter. Marylin had always assumed those girls—Rebecca Levin was one, Isabelle Burkett was another—baked cookies because they didn't have anything else to do. You could be sure Mazie Calloway wasn't going to call them up and see if they wanted to go to the mall for a mani-pedi.

But as she watched the snow drift down through the water and land on the ballerina's tulle skirt, Marylin wondered if Rebecca and Isabelle—and maybe Gracie McRae, for all she knew—baked cookies because they were good people. Really good. Not fake-smile good, not good so that everyone would like them good, but good because they had good hearts. Because they really wanted to help.

Marylin put the snow globe down on her desk. She'd spent her whole life having to choose sides.

Flannery or Kate? Mazie or Benjamin? She'd had to choose who to talk to in the hallways, who to pretend she hadn't seen. She had to choose who to smile at, which boys to say hi back to.

And in second grade, walking home from ballet with Gracie McRae, when Gracie had asked if she wanted to hold hands, Marylin had had to choose whether she wanted everybody in their class to think she was friends with the girl who stomped across the floor like a rhinoceros.

"My hands are cold," Marylin had told Gracie, quickly shoving her fists into her pockets. "Sorry."

"That's okay," Gracie had said. "I don't mind."

Marylin rushed out into the hallway. "Kate!" she yelled from the top of the stairs, even though she knew Kate was already out of the house. She ran down the steps two at a time. "Kate! Come back!"

Kate was standing on the front porch, her overnight bag at her feet.

"Why?" she asked Marylin, and Marylin was shocked to see that her eyes were filled with tears.

"Because," Marylin said, trying to catch her breath. "Because I need someone here with me when I tell Mazie no."

"Oh," Kate said. She wiped her eyes with the back of her hand and picked her bag up. "Okay. I can do that."

"I know," Marylin told her. "That's why I asked."

The two girls sat on the front step and waited. Marylin kept expecting Kate to change her mind, to stand up and tell her to forget it, she was going home. But Kate just sat there, writing invisible words on the sidewalk with a twig.

Ruby's sister, Marta, was driving the white SUV that pulled up to the curb in front of Marylin's house. Leave it to Ruby to have an older sister who seemed happy to drive her wherever she wanted to go, Marylin thought. No wonder she ruled the school.

As Marylin pushed herself up from the stoop, one the SUV's tinted windows slid down and Mazie's face appeared. "Get in the car!" Mazie yelled. "The salon closes in forty-five minutes."

"I'm not going, remember?" Marylin called back in what she hoped was a cheerful, oh-I-guess-we-have-a-tiny-misunderstanding-but-that's-okay tone. "I'm—I'm staying here with Kate. She's spending the night."

"You are insane," Mazie groaned. "Kate Faber is not coming with us, Marylin. That's out of the question."

Marylin expected Kate to say something, but Kate just kept writing stuff nobody could see on the sidewalk. She didn't even look up. Marylin was on her own.

"I'm not going with you either," Marylin said. She walked halfway down the front walk to the car. "I already have plans. I told you that."

Ruby Santiago's face appeared at the window next to Mazie's. "Then why are we even here, Marylin? You're wasting our time."

"I told Mazie on the phone I couldn't go," Marylin explained, flashing her best middle-school cheerleader smile at Ruby in hopes it would make her think of brand-spanking-new cheerleading uniforms. "I can't just abandon my neighbor to get a mani-pedi."

Ruby rolled her eyes. "Whatever," she said, and disappeared back into the car. "Let's go, Marta."

Marylin could feel Mazie's glare from ten yards away.

"Expect a text from me later!" Mazie yelled as the SUV pulled away from the curb. "This isn't over, Marylin!"

Marylin watched until they'd disappeared around the corner, then went back to the front porch. "You were a ton of help," she said, sitting down next to Kate. She pulled the twig out of Kate's hand and snapped in two. "Thanks a lot."

Kate shrugged. "It wasn't my fight. But you handled it pretty well, even if you called me a neighbor instead of a friend. I thought that was sort of weird and possibly insulting."

"I was just trying to make a point," Marylin insisted. "You're not just anyone. You're someone I grew up on the same street with."

"Uh-huh," Kate said flatly. "Well, I'll let it pass. I mean, like I said, you did pretty well for you."

"Wow, what a compliment," Marylin said,

throwing the pieces of Kate's twig into the grass. She knew she ought to feel good about doing the right thing, but mostly what she felt was doomed. Nobody said no to Ruby and Mazie. Nobody.

Uniforms, uniforms, uniforms, she chanted to herself. New uniforms would make everything okay. She turned to Kate, determined to keep things positive. "You don't want to give each other mani-pedis, do you?"

"Uh, I'm not sure that's really my thing," Kate said, but then she shrugged. "But sure, okay. Do you have any black polish?"

Marylin rolled her eyes. "Sure. I have a whole closet filled with black nail polish. It's just my style."

The two girls stood up. Kate brushed some pieces of grass off the back of her pants and said, "It could be your style. You could start a whole goth cheerleader thing."

Marylin just nodded and smiled, pushing Kate toward the front door. Everything was going to be okay. She'd get the squad new uniforms, and everyone was going to love her.

She'd paint Kate's fingernails a nice shade of raspberry and show her how awesome pink could be. All she had to do was keep smiling. All she had to do was keep pretending that everything in the world was fine.

On Tuesday morning Kate had left her lunch sitting on the kitchen counter, and now here she was in the cafeteria, face-to-face with a tray of brown and olive-green food. It was supposedly meat loaf and string beans, but Kate was not convinced.

"That should be illegal," Lorna said through a mouth full of pasta salad she'd made herself the night before. In her left hand she held a crusty piece of artisan bread, also homemade. "I can't believe the cafeteria is allowed to serve that kind of slop. I mean, look at it! All of the vitamins have been cooked right out of those beans. They're not even beans. They're bean remains. They could do a *CSI* episode on those beans."

"I've got to eat," Kate said with a shrug, half-heartedly sticking her fork into the slab of so-called meat loaf. "I've got a pre-algebra test this afternoon. I need the energy."

Lorna sighed and passed Kate her Tupper-ware container of pasta. "Just eat this, okay? I can't stand to watch you put that junk in your mouth. I can't believe they can't dish out some actual, fresh food. At my cousin's school, they have this amazing salad bar in their cafeteria. It's all stuff they grow in the school garden. How cool is that?"

"Pretty cool," Kate admitted. "We should do that here. There's lots of open space out on the student commons."

Lorna slammed her fist on the table. "We should! We should enter that competition! The one that Student Government is doing."

"The What's Your Big Idea competition?" Kate asked, and when Lorna nodded, she leaned back in her seat and thought about it. There was a lot about the idea of a school garden she liked. For one thing, a salad bar would be good for the school's vegans and vegetarians, who were always complaining about not having enough lunch options. Quite frankly, Kate could do with fewer cafeteria protests, especially since the leader of the vegans had gotten her hands on a bullhorn. And a school garden would be good for the environment, lower the school's carbon footprint and all that. She thought about Flannery and her do-it-yourself thing. She would totally be into a school garden.

"Let's do it," Kate said, grinning at Lorna. "I think it's a brilliant idea."

"We have to grow herbs, too," Lorna said, pulling a notebook and a pen out of her backpack. She started making a list. "Basil and tarragon would be totally great."

"Maybe we could grow chickpeas and make hummus. And garlic. We could grow garlic." Kate reached across the table and tore off a piece of Lorna's bread. "We could grow wheat for bread."

Without looking up from her notes, Lorna said, "I think you're starting to get carried away here, Kate, but I like your thinking."

"Me too," Kate agreed. "I am a very profound thinker."

"Incredibly, super profound," Lorna added, skewering a piece of rotini from the Tupperware container with her fork. "Most profound-from-on-high thinker."

Kate gnawed at the crust of her bread. "I wonder what the other ideas are going to be? Probably sports equipment for the gym and more computers for the library."

"Doesn't matter. Ours is the best. All we've got to do is submit it. Which means all you've got to do is write up the proposal."

Kate's mouth dropped open. "Me? Why me?"

Lorna smiled and handed Kate another chunk of bread. "No such thing as a free lunch, babe."

That night Kate sat at the kitchen table and worked on the school garden proposal. It had to be five hundred words or less, which was the sort of writing challenge Kate liked. She thought she should focus mostly on the food angle, since most middle schoolers she knew were obsessed with eating. Not the way Lorna was—she read *Bon Appétit* and could talk with authority about different kinds of olive oil— but just about everybody she knew was concerned with where their next snack was coming from and what it would consist of. If Kate *really* wanted to win this contest, she'd write a proposal for a new vending machine that dispensed only sour cream potato chips and kiwi-flavored bubble gum.

But Kate liked the idea of a school garden. She wasn't a gardener herself, but she could see how growing your own food was cool. Her mom usually had a few pots of cherry tomatoes growing on the patio, and it was always fun to take out a bowl and pick a bunch for a salad. It kind of made you feel like a farmer, or some kind of a hippie.

Her dad walked into the kitchen, carrying a plate. "Did you try some of Mom's raspberry pie?" he asked, putting his plate by the sink. "Amazing."

"You better rinse that plate off and put it

in the dishwasher," Kate warned him. "Mom's going ballistic every time she sees a dirty dish in the sink or on the counter. She says she's not our maid."

"She's not," Mr. Faber agreed. He reached over to turn on the faucet. "The problem is, she cares more than everyone else about the house being clean. I keep telling her she just needs to lower her standards."

Kate raised an eyebrow. "Yeah? And what does she say about that?"

"Nothing I can repeat in mixed company," Mr. Faber put his dish in the dishwasher, then sat across the table from Kate. "You working on homework?"

Kate told him about the What's Your Big Idea campaign and her and Lorna's proposal for a school garden. "I don't know if I should emphasize the importance of fresh food or tasty food."

"Go with taste, definitely," Mr. Faber advised. "I doubt kids care that much about freshness. You could take a 'tired of bland cafeteria food' approach, make everyone think about how much better their food could be. Don't worry about the vegetarians; you've got their vote already. Focus on the kids who have to eat cafeteria food every day. Would they rather eat some soggy broccoli or a great Caesar salad?"

"Do you think kids even care that much about salad?" Kate suddenly felt worried that no one would vote for her proposal because hardly anyone her age actually liked vegetables. She suspected that even the vegans didn't really like vegetables all that much; they just liked having something to argue about.

"Probably not, but people like what's new and different. You might also add a 'stick it to the man' element. Kids your age are starting to look for ways to rebel."

"Salad as rebellion," Kate mused. "I like it. You should have gone into advertising."

"I thought about it," Mr. Faber said. "I like messing around with language."

"Me too," Kate said. "I don't know why, I just do."

Kate's dad pushed himself away from the table. "Well, let me know if you need any more help. In the meantime, I might just sneak an extra slice of raspberry pie. Do you think your mom would mind?"

"I think if you put your dishes in the dishwasher, you can get away with murder around here," Kate told him.

After her dad left the kitchen, Kate stretched in her chair. She felt relieved all of a sudden, but she wasn't sure why. Because her dad had given her some good ideas for her proposal? She didn't think it was that. Maybe it was because they'd had a conversation where Kate didn't feel guilty or angry by the end of it. They'd had a conversation that had ended on a funny note instead of Kate's dad walking out of the room with a disappointed look on his face.

Disappointed over soggy broccoli? Kate wrote in her notebook. *Tired of depressed lima beans?*

She wrote as fast as she could, the ideas coming at her a mile a minute. It wasn't even that she was so excited about the idea of a school garden. It was more that she was excited about messing around with language. About making words mean what she wanted them to say. There was a trick to it, Kate knew, and she also knew that sometimes she was magic.

The next morning Kate couldn't wait to see Marylin on the bus. She thought Marylin was the perfect audience for her proposal—someone who was smart, big on school spirit, and okay with lettuce.

But before she got a chance to bring it up, Marylin was handing her a manila folder. "So I need you to tell me what you think about my proposal for the What's Your Big Idea contest. Do you think it's the sort of thing an average kid would vote for?"

Kate opened the folder and read Marylin's title: *Why New Cheerleading Uniforms Affect Everyone!*

She turned to Marylin. "You're kidding, right?"

"I'm not kidding at all," Marylin insisted. "Cheerleading uniforms matter. To everyone." She began ticking off the reasons. "They're important for school spirit. They're important for school pride. Studies show that when the cheerleaders are exceptionally cute, the teams perform better."

"You're making that up," Kate said. "That's totally bogus."

"I'm not making anything up," Marylin argued. "I might be paraphrasing a little bit, but that's different from making things up."

Kate handed back the folder. "This is so selfish! Nobody cares about your uniforms. And there's nothing wrong with the uniforms you guys already have. They're perfectly nice."

"'Perfectly nice' isn't good enough. Perfectly nice won't win us the district cheering championship, will it?"

Kate stared at her. Even Marylin wasn't this nuts, was she? "You're doing this so Mazie won't be mad at you, aren't you? For not going with her to the mall Friday night?"

Marylin flinched, and Kate knew she'd hit a nerve. "So what's she doing? Writing mean stuff on the bathroom walls?"

"She's not doing anything," Marylin said, examining her nails as though Mazie being mad at her wasn't a big deal. "Well, she's not talking to me, that's true. And some of the other girls aren't either, but that's just how they are. They'll get over it."

"Just as soon as you get them new uniforms, right?"

Marylin didn't say anything, but Kate could tell the answer was yes. She had two simultaneous, totally opposite feelings. She wanted to give Marylin a pat on the shoulder, like, *There, there, everything will be all right,* but she also wanted to punch her and yell, *Get a grip! Earth to Marylin! These people are not your friends!*

"I don't know, Marylin," she said, trying to sound nice about it. "I mean, do you really want to hang out with people who treat you like that? And also, do you think it's fair for someone who's on Student Government to submit a proposal? Isn't that, like, a conflict of interest or something?"

Marylin shrugged. "There's no rule that says I can't. And Benjamin said it was fine."

"Oh, that's right," Kate said, and now she was totally unable to keep the sarcastic tone out of her voice. "I forgot your boyfriend is president. I guess you've got this one in the bag."

"Actually, he's not all that crazy about my proposal," Marylin said, sounding worried. "I called him last night to go over it with him, but he acted like he didn't want to hear it. He probably just doesn't want to seem like he's playing favorites. Not that he actually has anything to do with which proposal wins. It's a democratic process, right? One person, one vote."

"And you think people are going to vote for cheerleading uniforms?" Kate snorted.

Marylin slipped the folder back into her back pouch. "I really do. You'd be surprised by how many students have true school spirit. Unlike some people I could name."

Kate took a deep breath and exhaled slowly. She hated the cheerleading side of Marylin. She hated how dumb it made her. Marylin could be goofy about a lot of things—that stupid flowered backpack she insisted on calling her back pouch, for example—but Kate liked Marylin's goofiness. The cheerleading thing was something else entirely. Dumb. It was just dumb.

They rode the rest of the trip in silence and didn't even say good-bye when they got off the bus, which made Kate feel bad, but she couldn't make herself be nice to someone whose big idea was getting more stuff for the kids who already had everything. How democratic was that?

She headed for the audio lab as soon as she got in the school's front door. Matthew would appreciate her proposal, she bet. He'd get how cool a school garden was. Matthew Holler was totally DIY.

"You are exactly who I wanted to see at this exact very minute," Matthew said when Kate found him working on his *World of Noise* recording. She felt her face flush and the tips of her fingers start to tingle. Really, she wished he didn't have this effect on her. It made everything between them so uneven.

"What did you want to see me about?" Kate asked, trying to sound cool. "Do you have a bridge you want to sell me?"

Wow, she thought, that sounded so *un*cool. She gave Matthew a lame smile. "Or something like that?"

"Something like that." Matthew grinned. "I have a project I want us to work on together. I want to enter that What's Your Big Idea contest and get some new gear for the audio lab. There's a new version of Pro Tools I've got to have, for one thing. And the soundstage needs a total upgrade."

"Uh, that's sounds really great and everything . . . ," Kate said.

"But?"

"But I'm kind of doing a proposal with Lorna," Kate told him. "For a school garden. So we can have—well, fresh lettuce at lunch and stuff like that."

Matthew looked disappointed, but he nodded at Kate and said, "Yeah, that's a totally cool idea too. I definitely get it. I'm just bummed because I thought this was something we could work on together. I thought we could go over to my house this afternoon, and you could maybe stay for dinner. My mom said it was cool, if you like spaghetti and garlic bread."

"I love spaghetti and garlic bread," Kate said, meaning it. She also loved hanging out at

Matthew's house, and she thought his mom was really nice, even if she had a rule about no girls in Matthew's room.

Matthew sighed. "Yeah, well, another time, right? So let me see what you wrote about a school garden."

"That's okay," Kate said. "It's not that interesting. I'm not even one hundred percent sure we're going to do it."

"So, then maybe you could work on the audio-lab proposal? I mean, at least help? Please?" Matthew made a face like a little kid pleading. "My mom makes killer garlic bread."

Kate found herself nodding. "Yeah, okay. Sure. I mean, the garden was really Lorna's idea. She can submit that proposal. They're both great ideas."

"They're both awesome ideas," Matthew agreed. "Too bad they both can't win."

Yeah, too bad, Kate thought, and then she thought how mad Lorna was going to be at her. How betrayed she was going to feel.

And then she thought about garlic bread, and how it was on her top ten list of reasons to live. Number one? Well, he was sitting on that chair over there, grinning at her.

Really, how could Kate say no?

"You're doing what?"

Lorna stared at Kate from across the cafeteria table. Her face was the shade of a homegrown tomato.

"I'm going to help Matthew with his proposal," Kate repeated. She reached into her backpack and handed Lorna the school garden proposal. "I worked on ours, and now I'm going to work on his. Just give him a little help. He wants to get some new equipment for the audio lab."

Lorna grabbed the proposal out of Kate's hand. "Oh! More stuff for the audio lab! Which already has everything! Which already sucks up all the school's extra money! And which maybe ten people use!"

"That's not true," Kate argued. "Everyone uses it. I had at least two audio-lab projects I had to do last fall."

"Yeah, that you *had* to do. People only use

the audio lab when they have to." Lorna rolled up the school garden proposal into a tube and smacked it against the table. "I've got a great idea—why don't we split the money between new cheerleading uniforms and new sound equipment for the audio lab? That way we ensure the fewest number of kids will benefit. I love that idea! It's the best idea ever."

Kate didn't even have to look up to know that people were staring at them. "Could you maybe turn the volume down to, like, nine? And could you quit destroying my proposal? I worked really hard on that."

"You worked hard on it, so now you're going to work hard on another proposal to compete against it?" Lorna asked in an only slightly quieter voice.

"They're two totally different things. They won't be competing against each other. If you're the kind of person who wants a school garden, you wouldn't even think about voting for the audio lab. It would be like the audio lab didn't even exist."

Lorna started packing up her lunch bag. "Do

you even hear yourself? You sound like—I don't know, a politician."

"Matthew's my friend!" Kate protested. "You're my friend. I just want to help my friends."

Lorna stood up and leaned across the table toward Kate. "I can't believe you don't get how much cooler a garden is than the audio lab! It's something a lot of people could be part of. Not just the kids who work in the garden, but the kids who would want to hang out there because it was a peaceful place. Or the artists, who could decorate it. It would be a place where people could play guitar or flute or whatever. Toss a ball around. It could be this great space in the middle of this crummy school. Not everybody would want to work in it or hang out there, but a lot more kids would want to hang out there than in the audio lab."

"Well, then, I guess everyone's going to vote for it, won't they?" Kate said in a tone of voice her mom would definitely call snotty. "So you don't have anything to worry about."

"No, I don't," Lorna said, and started to walk

away. She got only a few feet before she turned back around. "But you do. Because you are turning into the kind of person I'd bet a million dollars you don't want to be. Or maybe you do, which would be really sad. Really sad, Kate."

Kate watched Lorna stomp out of the cafeteria. She tried to remember why she was even friends with her. Maybe Lorna was jealous because Kate had a lot of friends and she didn't. All Lorna had besides Kate was her stupid *World of Warcraft* buddies, who weren't even real friends, they were online friends, which were just one step up from imaginary friends, in Kate's opinion. Kate couldn't help it if *she* was friends with Matthew and Flannery and Marylin—although maybe not with Marylin right that very second.

Whatever. Kate had friends, and she couldn't act like one friend was the most important, which was what Lorna wanted her to do. She wanted Kate to act like Lorna was the most important person in the world, and Kate couldn't. Sorry, but that's how it was.

Just think about garlic bread, Kate told

herself as she finished her sandwich. So she did. She thought about garlic bread and hanging out in Matthew's family room with his two dogs, Lemonhead and Ralph. Maybe she and Matthew would start hanging out at each other's houses all the time. One night they could do homework at Matthew's house, the next night they could do it at Kate's. Maybe Matthew would invite her along on his family's vacation next summer, and then he could come to the beach with the Fabers. Maybe they could start a band together and get famous.

The whole time she was thinking these things, another thought, a thought about kids hanging out in a garden, playing guitar, kept tapping against her brain, calling, *Let me in, let me in.* Kate shook her head. Nope, not thinking that thought, she told herself. It wasn't like she was suddenly against the school garden. In fact, she'd be happy if it won. But she couldn't put an idea in front of a friend, now could she? Matthew was more important to her than a school garden, because Matthew was her friend.

Kate's brain was starting to get tired. Who

was she arguing with? It felt like she was arguing with somebody, but Lorna wasn't here anymore, so who could she be arguing with?

She felt the answer forming itself in the back of her mind, so she shook her head really hard. She didn't want to think about it anymore. Enough thinking. She needed to start working on Matthew's proposal. What would make other kids vote for it? Kate looked around the cafeteria, sizing up potential voters. She should definitely go for the creative types and the computer geeks, make them see why the audio lab was the coolest place in the world.

She saw Marylin across the room at the cheerleaders' table. Nobody over there would vote for new audio-lab equipment, that was for sure. But just as Kate was about to look someplace else, she realized that Marylin was sitting at the very end of the table, and it almost seemed like she was sitting by herself, the way the other cheerleaders' chairs were at least two feet away from hers. Poor Marylin, Kate thought, and then she remembered Marylin's stupid idea for new cheerleading uniforms and decided not to feel sorry for her after all.

Maybe the audio-lab proposal should be entitled, *Vote for the Audio Lab, It's Better Than New Cheerleading Uniforms*. Which it was. Which was why Kate was not going to feel sorry for Marylin at all, even if she did at that very moment look like the loneliest person in the world.

The next morning on the bus to school, Kate sat as far away from Marylin as she could. Or was it the other way around? Either way, they were definitely ignoring each other. Well, who cared? It wasn't like what Marylin said or did mattered to her. She wasn't bothered by Marylin's silent treatment one bit.

No biggie. Whatever. Kate ignored the thought that now she was down to one friend. Why would she need more than one, anyway, especially if that friend was Matthew Holler? And so what if Matthew had kind of left the writing of the audio-lab proposal up to her? It made sense, really. Kate had already written one proposal; she knew what she was doing. So last night, she and Matthew had spent ten minutes brainstorming ideas for what Kate could say, and then they spent the rest of the time playing some game called *Kingdom Hearts: Birth by Sleep* on Matthew's PSP.

"I had another idea for your garden proposal," Kate's dad had said after she'd gotten home. She was sitting at her desk, putting homework pages into her various binders, and he was standing in her doorway with his iPad in his hand. "Are you still working on it? Or did you have to turn it in already?"

"Um, no and no." Kate had kept her eyes on her paperwork. "Lorna's sort of finishing it up. It's due Friday. I'm actually helping another friend with another proposal."

"So you're going to have two proposals competing against each other? Is that such a good idea?"

"It is what it is, Dad," Kate had said, sounding more irritated than she'd meant to. "I happened to have two different friends with two different ideas, and I wanted to help both of them. Why is that so horrible?"

Mr. Faber had walked over to the window and looked out. "It's not, I guess. I'm curious, though. Which idea are you going to vote for?"

"Um, I don't know," Kate had told him, and she didn't. She hadn't even thought about that yet. "They're both good ideas, but they're totally different from each other. One's the school garden, and the other is for money for the audio lab."

Mr. Faber had laughed. "Hasn't enough money been poured into that audio lab? Mac Warner from down the street told me he's been to professional recording studios that weren't as nice as your school's audio lab."

Kate had exhaled sharply. "Whose side are you on, Dad?"

"I don't know, Katie," her dad had said, turning to look at her. "I'd like to be on your side. Which side is that?"

"I don't know," Kate had mumbled. "I like both ideas."

Only she didn't, not really. She'd been telling herself and everybody else that she thought both ideas were great. But that wasn't true, was it? She thought a school garden was a great idea, and she thought Matthew Holler was a great idea. The audio lab? Sure, she liked it, and she liked that Matthew liked it, but it was just the sonic version of Marylin's cheerleading uniforms. Ten people would get something out of it, tops.

And then she remembered that Matthew was her friend, and Kate Faber was all about helping out her friends. After she put her homework binders into her backpack, she pulled out a pad of paper and her Pilot Precise V5 pen from her desk drawer and imagined being interviewed someday when she was a famous writer. "Do you write on a computer?" the interviewer would ask her, and Kate would say, "I always do my first drafts with pen and paper. It makes me slow down, so I can get exactly the right words." Really, Kate just liked office supplies, and she liked the way the right pen felt on the right paper. Strange but true facts about Kate Faber, she thought, and then she started writing down why the audio lab needed more money to pile on top of all the money that had already been invested in it.

After Kate had been writing for twenty minutes, she stopped and thought that maybe she should e-mail Lorna and see if everything was okay with the school garden proposal. She put down her pen and pad and opened up her laptop. After she sent the e-mail, she hit the send and receive all button approximately every three minutes, but Lorna never replied.

She probably went to bed early, Kate thought. She'll probably e-mail back first thing in the morning. Finally, around eleven, she turned off the computer. She read over what she'd written about getting new equipment for the audio lab. She was surprised by what a convincing case she'd made. It was a little scary, really. Because even though what Kate had written was good, she wasn't so sure she felt good about it.

What kind of person am I turning into? she wondered as she turned off her light and got into bed. The kind of person who helps out her friends, that's who. The kind of person who's there for the people who need her.

Sitting on the bus the next morning, ignoring Marylin as she read over her most excellent proposal for new equipment for the audio lab, she wondered if that was true. Was she really there for the people who needed her? And then she thought about going on vacation with Matthew Holler, and how she hoped they wouldn't go to the beach after all, because she was pretty sure she didn't want him to see her in a bathing suit.

To Kate's surprise, Lorna was sitting at their regular table at lunchtime. "Am I allowed to eat here?" she asked when she reached the table. "I have two pieces of my mom's famous raspberry pie. It's a couple of days old, but it's still good."

"It's a free cafeteria," Lorna said, sounding like she didn't care if Kate sat down or not. "It's not like I own this table."

"You never replied to my e-mail," Kate mentioned as she sat down and started unpacking her lunch. "I mean, even if you're mad at me, I did work really hard on that proposal."

"And it's really good," Lorna admitted, even though her voice was still chilly. "But you know what makes me so mad? I bet your proposal for the audio lab is really good too."

"I tried to make it less good, if that makes you feel any better," Kate confessed. "Only I couldn't. It would be like drawing a great picture and then tearing it up because you didn't like the person whose face you drew."

"It doesn't matter anyway. It's not going to win. Neither is a school garden, even if the proposal you wrote is great."

"Why not?" Kate said, feeling offended. How could one of her proposals not win?

Lorna dunked a pita triangle into a container of spinach dip. "Because someone told me that Jared Scott is doing a proposal for a big end-of-the-year pizza party. You know everyone's going to vote for that. Even if it weren't Jared Scott's idea, people would vote for it."

Jared Scott was the world's most popular eighth-grade boy. Lorna was right. Most kids she knew would sell their baby brothers for a pizza party. Not to mention that people would vote for his idea no matter what it was, just because they couldn't believe somebody as good-looking as Jared Scott sometimes actually smiled at them in the hallway.

"That's a bummer," Kate said, feeling suddenly like a halfway-deflated balloon. "Because a school garden's a truly awesome idea. I'm still going to vote for it."

Lorna stared at her. "You're not going to vote for the audio lab? Even though Matthew Holler would love you forever if you did?"

"Well, for one thing, it's a secret ballot," Kate said. "So he won't know what I voted for. And for another thing, I don't think he's going to love me forever. It's not really his style. And anyway, we're just friends."

"*He's* just friends," Lorna pointed out. "You're more, well—I guess it just seems like you care more. My mom says I shouldn't be surprised that you decided to help Matthew. She says a lot of girls do stuff like that to try to get a guy to like them."

Kate could feel her face go red. She hated the idea that Lorna and her mom had been talking about her! And that Lorna's mom thought Kate was like every other girl in the world, not to mention the kind of girl who would do stuff just to get a guy to like her.

"That's a really stupid thing to say," Kate said. "What does your mom even know about me?"

"She knows enough," Lorna said with a shrug.

Kate felt her throat tighten. I'm not going to cry, she told herself, and she focused on breathing slowly through her nose, a stop-crying trick she had come up with in elementary school. "He's my friend, why don't you get that?" she hissed at Lorna through clenched teeth. "Why doesn't anyone get that?"

Lorna looked at Kate for a long time. "I get it," she said finally, her voice soft. "But I'm your friend too." Now Lorna's eyes shone with tears. "So how do you think it made me feel when you started working on Matthew's proposal? It made me feel like I was a big, fat zero."

Well, there was no way Kate was going to stop herself from crying after that. The tears that rolled down her cheeks were hot, and Kate wondered if tears were always hot, or was it only the tears you cried because you'd been an idiot? A bad friend. The kind of girl who did things to get boys to like her.

"I'm sorry," she whispered.

Lorna sniffed and nodded. "Don't let it happen again."

Then they were quiet for a few minutes, until Lorna said, "Didn't you say something about raspberry pie?"

Kate laughed in a hiccupy sort of way and opened her lunch bag. "I even remembered to pack two forks."

"Wow, Martha Stewart would be proud," Lorna said admiringly. And then she said, "Is that Marylin sitting over there by herself? I've never seen her alone before. She looks weird all alone. Like she's missing an arm or something."

Kate looked up and sure enough, there was Marylin at a table near the cafeteria exit, sitting by herself and reading a magazine.

"Should we ask her to join us?" Lorna asked.

"You could split your piece of pie with her. I'm keeping mine all to myself."

"I don't know," Kate said. "Maybe she wants to be alone."

Lorna shook her head. "Nobody wants to be alone, Kate. At least not in the cafeteria."

Kate thought about this. She knew Lorna was right. She also knew that even if she thought Marylin was dumb for trying to get new uniforms to make Mazie like her, well, wasn't Kate sort of trying to do the same thing? Make Matthew like her by writing the audio-lab proposal?

She guessed Marylin wasn't the only person acting dumb around here.

Marylin gave her a little cheerleader-like wave when she saw Kate walking over to her table. "Hey! I'm just getting caught up on my reading for my current events journal!" She held up a copy of *Time* magazine.

"Why don't you come sit with me and Lorna?" Kate offered. "We can figure out how to take down Jared Scott. Maybe we could rig the ballot box."

Marylin sat very still for a moment, and then she began gathering her things. "You heard about that? Well, you're probably right—nobody else's idea has a chance. I guess it doesn't matter, though. I'm thinking about withdrawing my proposal anyway."

"Benjamin still mad at you?"

Marylin sighed. "Everybody's mad at me, Kate. Why am I so stupid?"

"Everybody's stupid sometimes," Kate told her. "So let's go eat some pie."

"Did your mom make it?" Marylin asked, looking considerably brighter.

Kate nodded and followed her friend across the cafeteria, to where her other friend was sitting. Outside the cafeteria window, she could see the student commons, where the leaves of a lone dogwood tree fluttered in the breeze. It would have been nice to have a garden out there, she thought. And then she thought that you didn't really need a lot of money to start a garden. Mostly you needed shovels and people to dig.

"How do you feel about lettuce?" she asked

Marylin, who looked at her like she thought Kate was crazy.

"I like it, I guess. I mean, who doesn't like lettuce?"

"Everybody likes lettuce," Kate agreed, and she wished like anything she had a writing pad and her Pilot Precise V5 pen. She wished she had a packet of seeds and a watering can. "You want to hear my big idea?"

Marylin rolled her eyes. "Can I have some pie first?"

Kate nodded. Pie was good. Eating pie with your friends while you planned a revolution?

Even better.

the crying game

Marylin thought maybe she should keep a list of all her stupid mistakes on her wall, just so she could keep track of them. The only problem with this idea was that you couldn't always tell what was a mistake and what wasn't. For instance, not going to the mall that night with Mazie—had that been a mistake or a step in the right direction? Well, she hadn't had much of a choice, had she? She couldn't exactly have left Kate alone at her house while she ran off to get a mani-pedi. So not going wasn't a mistake, but not having a good excuse? Big mistake.

If Marylin was going to be honest with herself, her real mistake had been inviting Kate over in the first place. She hated to admit that, but it was true. She should have kept her friendship with Kate strictly a bus friendship. No sleepovers, no hanging out on the weekends, just sitting together on the bus if that happened to be convenient.

Hurting Kate's feelings by telling Mazie the only reason Kate was at her house was to drop some stuff off? Superbig mistake, but Marylin didn't want to think about it, because when she did, she felt like a totally horrible person. And she really wasn't horrible—she just kept doing the wrong things over and over.

Marylin had been sprawled on her bedroom floor, drawing flowers on a school spirit poster, but now she sat up and leaned back against her bed. Okay, the number one biggest mistake she'd made lately? Trying to force Benjamin to get new cheerleading uniforms, even after her proposal lost. Which she knew was going to happen, she guessed, but she'd still been hopeful when Benjamin had read out the results of the What's Your Big Idea contest over the loudspeaker.

"And the third-place winner is . . . a new computer for the library!" Benjamin's voice had echoed through the hallway. Marylin was standing on the outskirts of the ring of cheerleaders by Ruby Santiago's locker, all of whom were rolling their eyes. Nobody believed the cheerleading uniform proposal was going to win, no matter how many times Marylin insisted it had a really good chance.

"In second place, a school garden!"

Marylin felt proud of Kate, though she felt a little annoyed, too, since she knew Kate and Lorna were going to go ahead with their garden plans even if the garden didn't win. They should have pulled out of the competition and let some of the other ideas—new cheerleading uniform ideas, for instance—get some of their votes.

"And the winner is . . ."

Marylin had crossed her fingers and her toes. Please, please, please, she'd thought. Let me have this one thing.

". . . a school-wide pizza party!"

Cheers had filled the air, along with shouts

of "Yes!" and "Awesome!" Ruby had glanced coolly at Marylin and shrugged. "Maybe you could still get us some new uniforms," she had said. "You've got Benjamin Huddle in the palm of your hand, right?"

"Sure," Marylin had told her. "No problem."

It turned out that only fourteen people had voted for new uniforms, which made it one of the least popular proposals; even the proposal for new audio-lab equipment had gotten more votes. But there was still going to be money left in the budget after the end-of-the-year pizza party. So why not uniforms?

"Because the money could be used for better things," Benjamin had insisted after Monday's Student Government meeting, when they were standing in front of the school, waiting to be picked up. "A lot of kids voted for a school garden, and there's enough money after the pizza party to at least get started on a garden. Mrs. Calhoun thinks it's a great idea."

"But it's not her decision," Marylin had pointed out. "It's kind of your decision, right? And it would mean a lot to me."

Benjamin looked uncomfortable. "Yeah, well . . ."

"Please?" Marylin said, trying to sound sweet, like a little kid asking for candy. Except it came out more like a desperate person who was pretty sure her whole world was going to collapse if she didn't get new uniforms for the cheerleaders.

Just then Benjamin's mom pulled up. "I've got to go," he said. "I'll see you—uh—I'll see you around, okay?"

That was Monday night. Now here it was Wednesday, and he hadn't called or replied to any of her texts or shown up one time at her locker.

"I guess that's that," Marylin said out loud, and started to cry. Again. For the ten thousandth time that week. Sometimes when she started crying, it was because of Benjamin, but after a few minutes she would start thinking about cheerleading, and then she was crying cheerleading tears.

Really, if she was going to be honest about it, the biggest, biggest mistake she'd made that week? Opening the e-mail with the subject header *50 Things We Hate About Marylin*. Sent from Mazie's phone, of course. There had actually been only seventeen things on the list, with number seventeen being "To be continued." Some of the things her fellow cheerleaders hated about Marylin included her hair ("dry and stringy"), her nails ("Ever heard of a pedicure?"), her breath ("Try brushing your teeth every once in a while!"), and her personality ("What a fake! Acts all nicey-nice, but is really super stuck-up").

Every item on the list felt like a little knife going into Marylin's heart. Why did they hate her so much? She was the nicest cheerleader in the whole group! She hardly ever talked behind anyone's back, and she was the only one who could do a double back walkover. Was that it? Did they hate her because she was flexible?

She'd told Kate about the e-mail the next day on the bus—another mistake, but in a week of big mistakes, a pretty tiny one—and to nobody's surprise whatsoever, Kate's advice was to quit immediately. "If you quit cheerleading, you could dedicate your life to Student Government and not have to spend your time with all those horrible people."

"But then I'd be a quitter," Marylin had pointed out. She didn't like quitters the same way she didn't like underachievers or people with bad attitudes. If you let go for just one minute, let yourself give up, who knew what would happen to you? You'd probably turn into somebody who wore her hair in a ponytail every day because—*meh, why bother?*

"But sometimes it's a good thing to be a quitter," Kate had argued. "It's good to quit smoking, right? Because smoking is harmful to your health. Well, I think cheerleading is harmful to your mental health. Just think about how you're being treated. It's not just e-mails. They're saying some really mean things about you at school. Lorna has PE with Mazie, and she's heard a lot of stuff."

Marylin had winced. "Don't tell me. I don't want to know."

"Okay, but it's not good. I mean, Mazie's telling everyone that you think you're better than everybody else in the school. That you're a total snob. Lorna stuck up for you, though. She said if you were such a snob, then why were you eating lunch with her?"

Marylin had closed her eyes and leaned her head against the window. Great. Not only did the cheerleaders hate her, they were making sure everyone else hated her too. She had to admit it: Mazie was a genius. She could just imagine the circle of girls leaning in toward Mazie as she told them how stuck up Marylin was. Mazie hardly ever talked to non-cheerleaders, so when she did, it was a big deal. Everybody listened. Everybody hoped that Mazie might swoop down and pick them for her friend, in spite of the million-to-none odds against that ever happening.

Now Marylin picked up a purple Magic Marker and leaned over the spirit poster again. She read what she'd written, blinked a couple of times, and read it again. Had she really written, *Go Maveriks!* instead of *Go Mavericks*? Really? Marylin lowered her head until the top of it was resting on the poster. Why was she so stupid?

I should just quit, she told herself, but she knew she wouldn't. Or couldn't. It wasn't about being a quitter or even about being popular. Okay, maybe it was a little bit about being popular. A lot about being popular. But there was something else, too—her parents sitting two rows behind the home team bench. It was like they were Marylin's cheerleaders, and when Petey came too, well, it was like they were a family again.

So Marylin couldn't quit. If she quit, when would her family ever get together? The five minutes at the door when her mom dropped her off at her dad's or her dad dropped her off at her mom's didn't count. Everyone being together in the gym, stomping their feet and yelling, eating hot dogs, making jokes?

That counted. And Marylin didn't want to ruin it.

"You know what you need?" Rhetta asked her on Thursday, when they were hanging out in Marylin's room doing their nails. Rhetta was finally off restriction, and she was taking advantage of it by spending every waking minute she could outside of her house. "You need more friends. Right now it's like you have your so-called cheerleader friends, and then you have your friends like me and Kate. Your weird friends. Not that Kate's actually all that weird, but you get my point."

"You're not weird either!" Marylin exclaimed. "I can't believe you'd even say that."

Rhetta looked up from where she was sitting, her back against Marylin's closet, a bottle of black nail polish in her hand. "I'm a preacher's kid, I dress all in black, and I'm in a bowling league. If that doesn't say 'weird,' I don't know what does. It's not a big deal. I like being weird."

"Well, anyway," Marylin said, deciding to ignore Rhetta's weirdo claims for the time being, "I have plenty of friends." She sat down on her bed and opened a bottle of pink polish. Sometimes she wondered what it would be like to paint her nails black, not that her mom would ever let her. Only she didn't really think she was a black-nail-polish girl at heart. In general, Marylin preferred the happy colors—pink, yellow, baby blue, spring green. Life was depressing enough without having depressing nails.

"Uh, no, you don't," Rhetta said. "You're known by a lot of people. In fact, I'd say almost every kid at school knows who you are. But just because they know you doesn't mean they're your friends. Really, what you need to do is dump the cheerleaders, make up with Benjamin, hang out with Kate and me, and then join a group. Like the Girl Scouts, maybe. Are we too old to be Girl Scouts?"

Marylin leaned back against her pillow, her knees pulled toward her chest, and began painting the nails of her right hand, which she was sort of terrible at, since she was right-handed. "I wanted to be a Brownie, but my mom had this rotten Brownie experience when she was a kid. Her troop leader made them do chores, like at her house. So she sort of discouraged me from signing up."

"Why don't you come to youth group with me?" Rhetta asked, blowing on the freshly blackened nails of her left hand. "It's not churchy at all, and everyone's nice. And the best thing? Only a couple of the kids go to our school, and they hardly ever come, anyway. So it would be like this fresh start for you. We wouldn't tell anyone you were a cheerleader or on Student Government. They'd get to know you just for who you are."

"But what if who I am is a cheerleader?"

Rhetta looked at Marylin for several long moments before speaking. "Marylin? In all honesty? You're not a cheerleader anymore. I think they're making that pretty clear."

Marylin took in a deep breath through her nose and slowly let it out. She stared at her toes, which she'd always thought were strange-looking. She kept hoping that one morning she'd wake up and they would be totally different, the big toe the biggest, the little toe like a nice, plump peanut. But every morning they were exactly the same, crooked and uneven. Just like her life.

I'm not going to cry, she told herself. I'm totally, completely not going to cry.

But she cried anyway.

. . .

Friday morning on the bus, Kate sitting beside her, Marylin thought about what Rhetta had said. Marylin was popular, but she didn't have many friends, and look at who her real friends were! Kate and Rhetta were great, but they weren't exactly normal. She guessed if she wanted to add another weird friend to the list, she could count Kate's friend Lorna.

Look at who your real friends are. Had Marylin really ever done that before? She went over the list carefully. Rhetta. Kate. Benjamin, maybe. Okay, and Lorna. That was it. How could that be? She was popular! She was pretty! How could she have only four real friends, and three of them weren't even normal people?

The bus pulled into the Brenner P. Dunn Middle School driveway. Marylin looked out the window at all the kids streaming through the open front doors. Really? Not one of them was her friend?

She turned to Kate. "I think I need to join a club. Maybe meet some new people."

"And quit cheerleading," Kate added. "Put that on your to-do list too."

"Could we focus here?" Marylin asked. "First, I think I'll sign up for something. And maybe I'll get to know some kids on Student Government a little better. There's just never time during the meetings to talk."

"How about Marguerite Holmes?" Kate asked. "She seems nice."

"That's not a bad idea," Marylin said, looking at Kate. "I'm surprised you even know who she is, though. I mean, she's pretty, well, mainstream."

"I am an observant human being," Kate said, sounding the tiniest bit offended. "I know who people are, even the so-called mainstream ones."

As it just so happened, Marguerite Holmes's locker was almost directly across from Marylin's, and Marguerite was there, pulling out books, when Marylin came down the hall.

"Hey, Marguerite! Are you ready for Student Government on Monday?" Marylin called in her best friendly, middle-school-cheerleader/ Student-Government-rep voice. "I think we're finally going to vote on the spring dance decorations!"

When Marguerite looked up and saw that it was Marylin talking to her, she didn't exactly look happy. She looked a little irritated, to be honest, like she didn't have time to deal with people like Marylin. Had Mazie gotten to her, too? Or was Marguerite the type of person who just naturally looked down on cheerleaders, even cheerleaders who were also Student Government representatives?

"It'll probably be the same thing as always—streamers and balloons," Marguerite said, turning back to her locker. "It would be great if we could do something different for a change."

"I totally agree," Marylin said. "It would be good if we had a more specific theme, not just 'spring dance.' I'm not saying this is a great idea, but we could do something like *Alice in Wonderland*. Or is that dumb?"

Marguerite shrugged. "It's not that dumb. I don't know if it's exactly right, but I get where you're going."

"Maybe we could eat lunch together today,"

Marylin suggested, smiling her best middle-school-cheerleader/Student-Government-rep smile. "Brainstorm a few ideas?"

"Sure, why not?" Marguerite said with a nod. "It would be good to go into Monday's meeting prepared."

Easy-peasy, Marylin thought as she crossed the hall to her locker. This making normal friends was a piece of cake. And when she opened her locker door to see that someone had dumped french fries and the remains of several cheeseburgers on top of her stuff, well, she was in such a good mood that she only cried a little bit. Just a few sniffs and a swipe of her eyes, and she was done.

Hanging out with nice girls was interesting. Not that Kate and Rhetta weren't nice. They were two of the nicest people Marylin knew, in their ways. Kate's kind of nice was gruff and maybe a little too much on the honest side, but it was nice all the same. Rhetta's niceness was true-blue nice that just happened to be buried under layers of black clothes.

But Marguerite Holmes's niceness was of the no-nonsense, straightforward variety.

"I'm only allowed three activities at a time," she told Marylin at lunch that day. "So right now I'm doing Student Government, horseback riding, and Service Club. I can't believe I got voted Student Government secretary this year. That's like a whole other activity, though I wouldn't tell my parents that."

"You're doing a great job," Marylin told her sincerely. "Being secretary is a lot of work."

"It really is!" Marguerite said, suddenly sounding more enthusiastic. "But it's surprisingly fun. It makes me feel like I'm really contributing to the school, you know?"

Marylin nodded. She did know. She also knew that if Mazie were listening to this conversation, she'd be rolling her eyes like crazy. Mazie was not the least bit interested in contributing to the school. She was more interested in what the school could do for her.

"Is this a private club?" Benjamin stood at the end of the table, holding a brown paper bag. "Or can anybody join?"

"What are you doing here?" Marylin asked, trying to sound nonchalant about it. She couldn't believe Benjamin was actually talking to her! "You don't have B lunch."

"I missed A lunch because I was at the dentist," Benjamin explained as he sat down next to Marguerite. "Mrs. Parker said I should just take B lunch, and she'd get me out of algebra."

Mrs. Parker was the school's administrative assistant, and as far as Marylin could tell, the most powerful person in the building.

Benjamin smiled at Marguerite. "Be prepared to do a lot of minutes-taking on Monday. It's going to be a long meeting."

"My mom's letting me bring her laptop," Marguerite told him. "I might audio-record, too, just to make sure I don't miss anything."

While Benjamin and Marguerite discussed what was on the agenda for Monday night's Student Government meeting, Marylin looked around the cafeteria. When she'd sat with the cheerleaders, she'd never looked around. Cheerleaders didn't look; they were looked at. It was sort of more interesting to look, Marylin thought now. You could learn a lot about the social world of Brenner P. Dunn Middle School by observing life in the cafeteria. The athletes and cheerleaders sat at the centermost tables. The geeks and losers and outcasts were dotted around the edges in groups of one, two, and three. Marylin looked around for Kate and Lorna, but they'd already left, probably to go to the audio lab. Marylin didn't know how she'd classify them. They weren't geeks and they weren't losers. What was that phrase her mom had used the other night at dinner, when they'd been talking about life without computers or electricity? *Off the grid.* Kate and Lorna were off the grid.

Marylin shivered. She would never want to be off the grid. But sitting here with Benjamin and Marguerite, two smart, friendly people who actually cared about doing some good in the world, well, it wasn't so bad. If the cafeteria was like a tree stump and you counted rings, Marylin's table would be in the third ring from the center. Looking around, Marylin took note of the other third-ringers. There were more Student Government reps, some chorus kids, a table of cross-country runners. Lots of band kids. People talked and laughed as they ate. Some kids were studying, and three tuba players were good-naturedly throwing food at one another.

It's not so bad here, Marylin thought as she dipped her spoon into her hummus. The question was, could she live here? Would people still think she was special and important?

"Do you need a ride Monday night, Marylin?" Marguerite asked. "Because I don't think I live that far from you. I remember from when I had to enter in everybody's addresses for the official Student Government record."

"That would be really nice," Marylin told her. "That way my mom wouldn't have to drag my little brother along when she dropped me off. He gets really cranky about having to come with us when my mom drops me off places. He thinks he's old enough to stay home by himself."

"My mom still won't let me stay home by myself," Marguerite said. "It's embarrassing, especially since I'm the oldest."

"I'm the oldest too, and my mom makes me babysit whenever she has to drive someone somewhere," Benjamin told them. "I've got four brothers and sisters, and it takes forever to load everyone into the van."

"My little brother backed our van down the driveway yesterday!" Marguerite exclaimed, laughing. "He's only three!"

They spent the rest of the lunch telling stories about dumb things their brothers and sisters had done over the years. As they stood up to take their leftover stuff to the trash, Marylin suddenly had a strange feeling. She couldn't put her finger on it. It was a butterfly sort of feeling, a spring morning kind of thing.

And then it hit her: She'd gotten all the way through lunch without crying. Not only that, but she actually felt sort of happy, like maybe her life wasn't falling apart after all.

She looked out the cafeteria window, where there were a few kids hanging out on the benches in the student commons. Turning toward Benjamin, she said, "I think a school garden's a good idea. You're right, it wouldn't take much money to get it started."

Benjamin grinned at her. "Seeds are cheap."

The three of them walked toward the exit. "You know, Marguerite, if we did an *Alice in Wonderland* theme, my parents could help us," Marylin said, this brilliant idea suddenly occurring to her. "My dad used to be this big theater guy in college, and my mom loves painting stuff."

"I was wondering, do you think we should do *The Wizard of Oz* instead?" Marguerite asked. "Or is that too creepy?"

"Too creepy," Marylin and Benjamin answered in unison, and then they both laughed, and Benjamin bumped Marylin with his shoulder, and she bumped him back.

Walking down the hall with her friends, Marylin thought that if they ever *did* have a dance with a *Wizard of Oz* theme, Mazie would make a great Wicked Witch of the West. And the rest of the cheerleaders? Flying monkeys. She thought they would make excellent flying monkeys.

• • •

When the doorbell rang Monday night, Marylin was still in her room getting ready. She checked the clock and saw that it was only six thirty. Marguerite and her mom weren't supposed to be there until six forty-five, though Marylin guessed she wasn't surprised that Marguerite was the sort of person who got places a few minutes early.

But when she opened the front door, it wasn't Marguerite. In fact, at first Marylin had no idea who it was. The pretty girl who stood on her front porch had reddish-brown hair in a cute pixie cut that made her brown eyes look enormous. She was wearing jeans and silver ballet flats, and a gray wool jacket over a pink sweater.

Marylin took a step back. And then she took two steps forward. "Rhetta? Is that you?"

Rhetta blushed. "Don't have a heart attack or anything."

Marylin started hopping up and down and clapping her hands. "I can't believe it! You look amazing! What happened?"

"Hmm, I think it's possible to take that

question the wrong way," Rhetta said, jamming her hands into her pockets. "Just maybe."

"You know what I mean," Marylin said, pulling Rhetta inside. "What did you do?"

Rhetta glanced behind her toward the street. "My mom's waiting in the car, so I can only stay a second. We're on our way to bowling league, but she said I could stop by really quick so you could see my hair."

Marylin couldn't help herself. She pulled Rhetta into a huge hug. "You look so amazing! Sorry! Sorry! But you do! Tell me what happened!"

Rhetta broke away and sat down on the stairs. "Okay, okay! Let me catch my breath! Well, here's the thing. I've been really worried about you."

"So you cut your hair?"

"Sort of, yeah," Rhetta said, nodding. "See, where I used to live, in sixth grade, there was this girl at our church, Lacey Griffins, who got cancer. She had to go through six months of chemotherapy and lost all her hair. So all the guys in the youth group shaved their heads, to show solidarity, and two of the girls did too."

Marylin sat down next to Rhetta on the stairs. "That's awesome," she said. "But I still don't get why you cut your hair."

"Okay, so maybe you don't have cancer," Rhetta said, turning to look at Marylin. "But things have been really terrible for you. Not just cheerleading, but your parents getting divorced and you having to go back and forth all the time between their houses, all that stuff. Things just seem so hard for you. I was talking to my mom about it, and she asked me what kind of friend you needed me to be right now. And suddenly I got this idea. I thought you needed me to be—" Rhetta's voice caught, like she was about to cry.

"What do I need you to be?" Marylin asked. "Tell me."

"You need me to be normal," Rhetta said, and now she was crying for real. "You need me to be less of a weirdo for a little while."

Now Marylin was crying. "You are not a weirdo! Don't say that!"

Rhetta grinned through her tears. "I'm sort of a weirdo. I mean, I *am* in a bowling league.

You can't get around that fact. But in a lot of ways I'm also a pretty normal person."

"I know you are," Marylin said, nodding vigorously. "I've always known you were. You were just hiding it."

"Well, anyway," Rhetta continued, wiping her eyes and sniffling. "When I told my mom, she just went nuts, she was so happy. She took me clothes shopping, and we went to her favorite Christian hairdresser—"

"There are Christian hairdressers?"

"Oh, yeah, there's Christian everything," Rhetta told her. "Anyway, believe it or not, this is pretty close to my natural hair color. I'd sort of forgotten, but my mom brought pictures."

"You didn't have to do this for me," Marylin said, leaning into Rhetta. "I always thought you were great."

"That's why I did it," Rhetta said, leaning into Marylin. "You're the first friend I've ever had who always thought I was great, even when you thought I was weird."

Outside, a horn honked. "That's my mom," Rhetta said, standing. "I've got to run. But believe me, you're going to love what I'm wearing tomorrow. More pink!"

Marylin watched as Rhetta headed down the sidewalk. "Hey, Rhetta," she called after her friend. "You know what?"

"What?" Rhetta called back as she opened the car door.

"I think I'm going to quit cheerleadering. At least for now."

"Good," Rhetta said. "They don't deserve you. See you tomorrow!"

Marylin hurried back inside to wash her face and fix her hair before Marguerite got there. Just because she wasn't going to be a cheerleader anymore didn't mean she wasn't going to do her best to be pretty. Pretty was part of who she was, even as a soon-to-be civilian.

Would she tell Marguerite that she was quitting her life as a middle-school cheerleader? Should she announce it at the Student Government meeting? She thought it would be nice to see people's faces when she told them. She liked the idea that other people would be on her side, that maybe most people were on her side. That she had more friends than she knew.

Looking in the mirror as she brushed her hair, Marylin wondered if the girl in Rhetta's church, Lacey, had gotten better. Suddenly it seemed important to her that Lacey was okay. That all those boys and the two girls shaving their heads—well, that it had made a difference. That having friends made a difference.

Marylin looked at her reflection. Of course having friends who would shave their heads for you would make a difference. How could it not?

The doorbell rang, and Marylin grabbed her coat and opened the front door. "I'm thinking about cutting my hair," she told Marguerite as she stepped onto the porch. "What do you think?"

Marguerite laughed. "I think you'll look great whatever you do."

"My best friend has short hair," Marylin explained. "That's what got me thinking about it."

She slid into the car and snapped her seat belt into place.

She felt better already.

free as a girl with wings

On Tuesday night, after she'd finished her math homework, Kate turned on the radio and sprawled across her bed, waiting for a song that would change her life. She did this every night after she finished her homework; it had become part of her routine. Some nights she didn't have any luck at all—heavy metal night in particular offered pretty slim pickings—but Tuesday was the *Girls with Guitars* show, and the odds were pretty good that she'd hear at least one song that would blast through all the noise in her brain and make her sit up and say, *YES! That's it! That's exactly it!*

The first two songs the deejay played were

pretty lame. One was about how the singer would never meet another guy like the one who'd just dumped her, and even though Kate was only thirteen, she knew there'd be plenty more guys just like the one who got away. Boring. The second song was about baking bread. Now, Kate liked freshly baked bread as much as the next person, and she thought you should be able to write about anything you wanted, but that didn't mean you could rhyme words like "orange" and "curtain"—words that, frankly, didn't rhyme at all—and get away with it.

But the next song was a girl singing about looking for a new life, a life where she could be exactly who she wanted to be, and maybe she'd find that life in another town, maybe in another country, she didn't know. Listening to the girl sing, Kate thought, YES. That was exactly what she wanted too.

Not that Kate really wanted to move to another town, at least not right this very minute. Eventually she'd probably move to New York City and live in Greenwich Village, although when she'd mentioned that to her dad, he'd laughed and said she'd better grow up to be a millionaire. Secretly Kate thought that she'd rather go up to New York with only twenty dollars in her pocket. It would make a better story when she became a famous singer-songwriter, or a famous poet, or whatever she ended up being famous for, if she showed up in New York totally broke. She hadn't said this to her dad, though. He was too practical to like that kind of idea.

After the song was over, Kate grabbed her notebook and started to write. *Free. Free as a girl with wings. Free as the grass that grows without anyone telling it to. Free as a person who gives everything away and keeps on walking.*

Kate was in love with the idea of being free, even if she was having a hard time pinning down exactly what it meant. It had something to do with not caring what other people thought, and she liked that idea a lot. She was tired, for instance, of caring what Matthew Holler thought. She was tired of getting dressed in the morning and wondering if Matthew would like what she was wearing. She hated wondering that! And she hated how, if she didn't see Matthew in the audio lab or at his locker first thing in the morning, she felt disappointed, like how could her life have meaning if she didn't see Matthew before first period?

So on Tuesday night she decided she was going to give Matthew Holler up. She was going to stop caring about him. Sure, they could be friends, but Kate thought it was time to have other guy friends too, maybe even a boyfriend. There was a guy in pre-algebra named Keller Knowles who seemed pretty cool. He wore cool T-shirts, anyway, and he acted kind of shy, which was a trait Kate thought was nice.

But would she be free if she had a boyfriend? Kate would have to think about that.

Wednesday, during morning break, she decided to go to the audio lab one last time. It would be her farewell to Matthew Holler, her hello to freedom. She pushed open the door, feeling strong and powerful, and maybe just a little sad. It was a cool combination of feelings, and she was pretty sure she could write a song about it later.

And then, when she saw Emily sitting next to Matthew at the control panel, giggling and poking him with her pencil, Kate thought she might be writing a whole different kind of song. Not that Matthew was poking Emily back or acting like he was in love with her. It was just—well, he let Emily sit in Kate's chair. Like it didn't matter who was sitting there. Emily? Kate? What was the difference? Who cared?

As soon he saw Kate, Matthew said, "What's up?" Kate thought he sounded entirely too nonchalant, like, *Oh, is my ex-girlfriend hanging out with me? I hadn't noticed.*

Emily smirked and said, "I'm helping Matthew with his project. It's called *World of Noise*, and it's really cool."

"I know what it's called," Kate said, and she waited for Matthew to explain to Emily that Kate had been working on the project with him for two months now, and of course she knew what it was called. But Matthew didn't say anything. He just kept fiddling with the levers on the control panel.

Not a big deal, Kate told herself as she turned around and headed out the door. In fact, it was good that Emily had been there and that Matthew had acted like Kate wasn't anybody special. It made it that much easier to give him up. And the fact that she sort of felt like crying? Well, that was going to happen, wasn't it? Just because she wanted to stop caring about Matthew Holler didn't mean it would happen automatically. It would take practice. She just had to keep practicing.

Kate decided she would go work on painting sets for *Guys and Dolls* with Lorna. Maybe she could even get Ms. South, the drama teacher, to give her a pass to get out of fourth period. The only question was, should she tell Lorna about finding Emily in the audio lab, or her decision to get over Matthew? Kate shoved her hands in her pockets. For some reason they were shaking a little. The decision. She should definitely talk about the decision first. Emily was beside the point.

When she got to the auditorium, she found Lorna and Flannery painting the Save-A-Soul Mission storefront. Over the last few weeks, Lorna and Flannery had gotten to be friends. It had a lot to do with the amazing snacks Lorna brought to rehearsal and the fact that Flannery wasn't half so cranky if you fed her.

"Pick up a paintbrush," Lorna called when she saw Kate. "We've got ten minutes before break's over."

"Yeah, Ms. South wants this finished and all the way dry by rehearsal this afternoon," Flannery added.

It was interesting to see Flannery so involved, Kate thought. Flannery was not known for being an overachiever when it came to activities. The other day she'd told Kate and Lorna that the only other times she'd after stayed after school were for detention. "This show is the first time I've voluntarily stayed at school one second longer that I absolutely had to."

"Doesn't your mom care about extracurriculars?" Lorna had asked. "Because my mom has a total bug up her butt about them."

Kate had noticed that the longer Lorna hung out with Flannery, the more she was using phrases like "bug up her butt." Flannery was the sort of person who could have that kind of effect on your vocabulary.

"Mostly my mom just cares that I get out of middle school without a police record," Flannery had informed them. "Not that I actually do anything all that bad. I guess I just have potential when it comes to a life of nonviolent crime."

"You look weird, Kate," Lorna said now as Kate picked up a paintbrush and started working on the mission's front door. "Are you okay? You're not going to throw up, are you?"

"I'm fine," Kate said. "I just have some big news that I'm very excited about. I've decided I'm done with Matthew Holler."

Both Lorna and Flannery looked skeptical. "What do you mean by 'done'?" Lorna asked. "Like you're going to stop hanging out with him?"

"Or stop obsessing about him?" Flannery added.

Kate scowled. "I don't obsess about Matthew Holler. That's dumb."

Now Lorna and Flannery rolled their eyes in unison. "Kate," Lorna said, and Kate could tell she was trying to sound gentle, but not trying all that hard. "You spend every free minute of your day hanging out at the audio lab, listening to that awful *World of Noise* project Matthew's working on. You drop his name into every conversation, like, 'Oh yeah, when I was hanging out at Matthew's the other day . . .' You're totally obsessed."

"Well, not anymore," Kate insisted. "I need to be free. I'm tired of someone else controlling my life."

Flannery looked at Lorna. "Finally."

Lorna nodded at Flannery. "It's about time."

"Have you guys been talking about me?" Kate clenched her fists. She *hated* when people talked about her! "Like, gossiping about me and Matthew?"

"It's helped cement our friendship," Flannery said with a shrug.

"It's only because we care," Lorna added.

"Well, I guess now you're going to have to find something else to talk about," Kate said, sounding huffy. "Because Matthew Holler will no longer be a topic of conversation." She turned to Lorna. "So what kind of snacks did you bring today?"

"You're just using me for food," Lorna said, but she sounded happy about it. Lorna loved being famous for her cooking.

What if all Kate was famous for was being that girl who hung out with Matthew Holler? If she got hit by a truck this afternoon, was that how people would remember her? *Oh yeah, Kate Faber—she was the one who had that thing for Matthew. She was the one who followed Matthew Holler around like a puppy.*

Kate felt her face go red. How had she become that sort of person?

Well, she wasn't that sort of person anymore. From now on, she was the sort of person who wore what she felt like wearing, said what she felt like saying, and did what she felt like doing. She was the sort of person who was known for being independent and outspoken.

That Kate Faber, people would say, *she doesn't care what anybody thinks. She just does exactly what she wants.*

Yep, that's me, Kate thought, taking a swipe at the mission door with her paintbrush. Free as a bird. Free as a comet. Free as the Fourth of July.

Kate was sitting on her bed that night, writing in her poetry notebook, when her dad came to the door, the phone in his hand. "Matthew called when you were in the bathroom earlier. He said to call him back when you got a chance."

"When I was in the bathroom? Like, thirty minutes ago? And you're just telling me now?"

Mr. Faber nodded. "I was on the phone with a client. I tried to ignore the call-waiting beep, but it kept going off until I finally couldn't stand it anymore."

"You know, if you'd let me get a cell phone, we wouldn't be having these problems," Kate pointed out. Her dad was totally against his children having cell phones. He had a folder full of articles about how cell phones gave you brain cancer. It was in his file cabinet, right next to the folder where he kept all his clipped newspaper articles about teenagers dying in drunk-driving accidents.

"Not going to happen, Katie. We'll just have to keep living like primitives." Mr. Faber held up the phone like he was about to toss it to her. "You want to call him back? I'm done with my business."

Did Kate want to call Matthew Holler? How was she supposed to answer that question? Of course she wanted to call him! She wanted to call and ask him if he'd heard the new Midtown Dickens song on K-DUCK, the one where somebody played a saw, and how cool was that? She wanted to call and tell him about this book of poems she'd just checked out of the library, *Reflections on a Gift of Watermelon Pickle*. She wanted to call and read him a draft of the poem she was working on, which she was calling "Free as a Bird Who Just Discovered It Was Free."

The only problem was, the poem was sort of about being free from Matthew Holler.

"I'll see him at school tomorrow," Kate told her dad. "It probably wasn't anything important."

Mr. Faber gave Kate a long look. "Everything okay? Between you and Matthew, I mean?"

"There is no me and Matthew," Kate insisted. "He's just a friend. There's nothing between us. That makes it sound so—I don't know, just not what it is."

Her dad leaned down to pull at a piece of tape stuck to the carpet. "I thought maybe he was—you know, your boyfriend."

Kate thought she might throw up. "Dad! I don't want to talk about this stuff! Do you have these kinds of talks with Tracie? Like, about who her boyfriend is?"

"Tracie hasn't spoken to me in three years," Mr. Faber said. "Except to ask me for money, or for a ride to the mall. But a substantial conversation about her actual life? Nope. Hasn't happened."

Now Kate felt guilty. Why did her dad always make her feel guilty? Like she was a terrible person, just because she didn't want to play basketball on Saturday mornings or talk about her love life?

"Maybe you and Mom should have another baby," Kate said, doodling in her notebook. "Maybe this time you'd get a boy, and you guys could have lots of personal, manly talks about, I don't know, antifungal cream."

Mr. Faber snorted. "One, I'm not sure your mom would think that was such a hot idea. Two, even if we have a hundred more babies, I'd still want to know about you, Katie. I know it's not going to be the way it was when you were five and wanted to tell me every single thing that happened to you. I know you have to have your own life—"

Then, abruptly, he shut up. He rubbed his eyes, and Kate thought her dad might be on the verge of crying. Oh, please don't let him cry, she begged silently. Please, God or the universe or whoever's out there, don't let him cry. Kate was pretty sure that if her dad started crying, she would break into a hundred little pieces and no one would ever be able to put her together again.

"Listen, I know you're growing up," Mr. Faber began again. "I get it. And your mom says I should give you a lot of space, which I'm trying to do. I just always thought—"

"Always thought what?" Kate urged, hoping that if her dad kept talking, he'd be less likely to have an emotional breakdown.

Mr. Faber sighed. "That we'd always have a good relationship. That you'd stay my pal."

Kate tried to make herself say it. She tried to make herself utter the words *I am your pal, Dad.* But she couldn't do it. All she could offer was, "I'll tell you some stuff, okay? Like, I could tell you about play rehearsal. Lots of interesting stuff happens at play rehearsal."

"That would be great," Mr. Faber said. He nodded toward her desk chair, as if to ask, *Mind if I take a seat?* Kate gave him a magnanimous wave, as if to say, *Sure, why not?*

"You know, I worked on the tech crew for some musicals in high school," her dad said as he crossed the room. "*Bye Bye Birdie, Fiddler on the Roof.* Never *Guys and Dolls*, though."

"It's a lot of fun," Kate told him. "Well,

except when Ms. South makes us do a song ten million times."

Mr. Faber was about to sit down when the phone in his hand rang. "Probably Matthew again," he said, holding out the receiver to Kate. "You want to take it?"

Kate took a deep breath. "No, that's okay. Let the machine pick it up."

"Good girl," her dad told her, and Kate sat back, surprised. The way he said it? It sounded like he knew exactly what she was thinking, that if she took this call, she'd take the next one and the next one and the next one. And if she kept taking Matthew's calls, she'd never be free. She'd never be the bird in her poem.

"I'm trying," she told her dad. "It's hard, but I'm trying."

Her dad nodded, and Kate realized they'd just had a conversation about her personal life without actually talking about it.

Works for me, she thought.

The problem was, Matthew Holler kept waiting for her at her locker. It was funny how now that she wasn't going out of her way to hang out with him, he seemed to be waiting around for her a lot more. It sort of made Kate mad, to be honest, like Matthew was playing games with her. She was pretty sure that if she started showing up at the audio lab every morning, Matthew would go back to his old routine, where sometimes he seemed really happy to see her, and other times he acted like he couldn't care less.

And it was weird that something Kate used to actively wish for on a daily basis—that Matthew would be waiting for her at her locker, which he almost never had been—had turned into something she sort of dreaded. As soon as she saw Matthew at her locker, she felt self-conscious, and she was tired of feeling self-conscious. She was tired of spending 99 percent of her time worrying that she should have flossed after breakfast. She bet that Walt Whitman or Amelia Earhart never worried about that kind of stuff.

"But you like it, too, don't you?" Flannery asked after Kate complained at play rehearsal one afternoon. "It's kind of cool that he's waiting for you, right?"

"Yeah, sort of," Kate admitted. "I guess it means he cares."

But that was the real problem, Kate decided after thinking about it for a while. Matthew Holler cared, even if sometimes he acted like he didn't. He thought that he and Kate were still friends. And they *were*, only Kate kind of needed a friendship vacation. She needed a few weeks, maybe a month, to practice not caring. To practice thinking her own thoughts without wondering if Matthew had the same sort of thoughts, or if he would think her thoughts were stupid or obvious or uncool.

"You need a boyfriend," Marylin advised her on the bus one morning. "You need to have another boy waiting at your locker. Guys are super territorial. Believe me, if Matthew sees a guy at your locker, he'll back off."

"But I don't want a boyfriend," Kate complained.

"So, get somebody to pretend he's your boyfriend," Marylin suggested. "At least for a week or two. I bet if I asked Daniel Wyncoop to do it, he would. Do you know him? He's on the spring dance committee, and the other day he asked me for advice about girls. He's pretty shy. You could be a practice girl for him, and he could be a fake boyfriend for you."

"Wow, that might be your worst idea yet," Kate said, reaching into her backpack for a pen. "I'm going to start making a list, and at the end of the school year we'll compare and contrast."

Marylin punched her in the arm. "Stop! My ideas are great. Okay, well, if you don't like my fake boyfriend idea, how about this—why don't you quit going to your locker first thing in the morning? Pack your first-period stuff the day before, and then in the morning you don't have to go to your locker until second period. Maybe if you don't show up for a few days, Matthew will start to think you have a boyfriend, and he'll leave you alone."

The idea of Matthew leaving her alone made Kate sad, but she had to admit Marylin's idea might actually work. "I just want to take a break from him. Just for a little while."

"Yeah, I get that," Marylin said. "Not that I want to take a break from Benjamin or anything. At least, I don't think I do. Everything's just weird right now. I'm trying to reprioritize my life, now that I'm not a cheerleader anymore."

"Do you think that Benjamin cares? I mean, that you quit?"

Marylin stared out the window. "Maybe a little? I think he liked the whole cheerleader mystique thing."

Kate almost said something sarcastic, but she decided not to. It was a big deal that Marylin had quit the squad, and Kate felt like she ought to be as supportive as she could.

"Maybe he's just getting used to the new you," she proposed. "It took a lot of guts to quit. Maybe Benjamin didn't know what kind of woman he was really dealing with."

"Or maybe Mazie's telling him terrible things about me," Marylin countered. "Who knows?"

"Benjamin wouldn't listen to Mazie. He's too smart for that. Really, I don't think you should worry about him."

"Really?" Marylin looked at Kate, her expression torn between hope and fear.

"Really," Kate assured her, and was surprised by how relieved Marylin looked. A lot of people probably thought that being pretty would protect her from worrying about whether her boyfriend liked her, but Kate knew Marylin well enough to know it didn't.

That's why I want to be free, Kate told herself as she walked inside the school building and headed toward her locker. If you like somebody, they have too much control over you. Who wants that?

Matthew was waiting for her. Why was he there, morning after morning? Did he miss Kate adoring him all the time?

"I wish I could hang out and talk," Kate said when she reached her locker. She began working the combination. "But I have to go meet someone. I have to go meet this—this guy I know."

"Oh yeah?" Matthew sounded like he was trying not to sound too interested. "Who's that?"

"Just this guy. He's, uh, nobody." Kate tugged at her earth sciences notebook, and Matthew reached over her shoulder and pulled it out for her. "Thanks," she said. "Stuff just sort of gets wedged in there."

Matthew looked to his left, then to his right, like he was checking for spies. Then he leaned toward Kate and said, "Are you mad at me or something?"

"Why would I be mad at you?" Kate asked, shoving her books into her backpack. "I can't think of any reason."

"Me either," Matthew agreed. "It's just, you don't call me anymore or come to the audio lab. And you haven't written me a note all week. You know, 'Who's greater, Jack White or Jack Johnson?'"

"That's stupid," Kate told him. She zipped her backpack closed. "I would never do one that stupid. *Curious George* Jack Johnson? Really?"

"No, not really," Matthew said, his cheeks reddening. "It was just an example. I just don't think you should be mad at me."

"I'm not mad at you," Kate said, trying to sound as grown-up as possible. "I'm really, truly not. I just have a lot going on. You know, the musical and everything, and I'm writing a lot. And you're busy too, with *World of Noise*. It's just a busy time."

"You sound like my mom," Matthew complained. "Next thing you'll be telling me you have to go to your book club meeting right after you make brownies for the PTA bake sale."

"That's exactly what I was going to tell you next," Kate said. "How'd you guess?"

Matthew snorted. "Quit, okay? Just quit being mad at me and quit being sarcastic and quit thinking that just because Emily is hanging out in the audio lab that it means anything."

"I don't care about Emily hanging out with you," Kate said, which was a lie, but it was a lie she wanted to believe more than anything in the world. "Why would I care?"

Matthew leaned toward Kate's locker and slammed the door shut. "You care because you care. You can't help it. And I care, okay? In case you were wondering."

Kate didn't know what to say. She stood there for a minute, staring past Matthew's left shoulder. "But I don't want to care," she said finally. "And that's why I need you to leave me alone."

"What?" Matthew looked at her like he couldn't believe what she was saying, his cheeks getting even redder. "You want me to *what*?"

Kate thought that he looked like he was about to cry, and maybe she was wrong about that, but she turned around and walked away anyway. Why is everything so stupid? she thought, walking into the girls' room at the end of the hallway. Why is it so dumb? she wondered, locking herself in a stall and just standing there for a long, long time, until everything stopped hurting long enough for her to go to the office and ask them to call her house because she didn't feel so good and needed to go home.

Kate's dad picked her up in front of the school. "Good thing I was working at home today, huh?" he asked as Kate slid into the front seat. "Your mom would have come except for that whole cupcake thing."

"Yeah, the Garden Club luncheon. I can't believe I forgot about that."

"Two hundred fifty cupcakes for seventy old ladies," Mr. Faber said, shaking his head. "I don't know, that seems extreme to me. So how's your stomach? Do we need to stop at the drug store for some Pepto?"

Kate had told the school nurse she had a bad stomachache. Stomachaches were her go-to excuse for getting out of school. You could have a stomachache and still have a normal temperature, not to mention that as soon as you said your stomach hurt, everyone got immediately concerned you were going to throw up. The throw-up factor packed quite a punch, in Kate's experience.

"I think I just need to eat some toast or something," Kate told her dad. "Just something to settle my stomach down."

"Maybe we should stop at Elmo's on the way home then. I don't think Mom's letting anyone in the kitchen right now. It's cupcake central in there."

Elmo's was the diner where Kate and her dad used to go after they played basketball on Saturday mornings. Mr. Faber always ordered a cheese omelet and an extra-large orange juice. For a while, Kate had been methodically working her way through the breakfast menu, but had given up when she got to the tofu and sprouts frittata. After that, she usually just got strawberry yogurt with granola and a Danish.

Kate had never been to Elmo's on a weekday morning and was surprised to see how busy it was. "Breakfast rush," her dad said as he pushed open the door. "Expect to hear the clatter of silverware."

A waitress guided them to a booth, and as she took her seat Kate heard what her dad meant. It was like a symphony of spoons tapping against coffee cups and forks scraping plates. "It would be so cool to record this," she told her dad as the waitress handed them their menus. "Matthew could totally use it for his *World of Noise* project."

As soon as she said it, she wished she hadn't. The sad feeling started in her stomach and then it covered her all over, inside and out. In a weird way, it seemed like Matthew had died. He's gone away from me, she thought, and then, because she was a poet and a songwriter and couldn't help herself, she thought, My baby's done gone away, done gone away from me.

"You know what I'd do if you were a guy— I mean, a grown-up guy?" Mr. Faber asked, and Kate shook her head no. "I'd say, 'Let's go out and play some hoops and then go grab a beer.' I realize that's a totally inappropriate response to a thirteen-year-old girl who's feeling blue, though. Well, not the hoops part. Maybe instead of a beer, I could buy you a jelly doughnut?"

Kate shrugged. "A cheese Danish might be nice."

"Your stomach up for it?"

"I'm starting to feel a little better, I guess."

Her dad grinned from across the table. "I bet nobody's on the court at the Y right now. We could have it all to ourselves."

"I don't know, Dad. I mean, my stomach's

feeling better, but I don't know if I want to play basketball."

"Okay, here's another idea. We get our Danish to go, and we drive around town with the radio turned up all the way—any station you want—and then we go shoot some hoops."

"You really think that will help?" Kate asked, having her doubts. What if her dad wanted to listen to Bon Jovi on the radio? Or even worse, Rush?

Her dad lifted his arms into the air, like a wild-eyed preacher on TV. "We'll roll down the windows and sing loud as thunder! We'll play air guitar like rock gods! It'll be like we're teenagers again, free from worries and woe!"

Kate looked around nervously, but no one seemed to be paying attention. "Um, Dad? I'm still a teenager. In fact, I just started being a teenager a couple of months ago."

Mr. Faber nodded his head knowingly. "Yes, but you are full of worry and woe, are you not? And you'd like to be free from it, am I right?"

What could Kate do but say yes? She *was* full of worry and woe, after all, not to mention that she had a heavy heart and a head full of broken dreams. *My baby's done gone, and now I'm sad and blue*, she sang to herself. But that wasn't even right, was it? It should be, *I done gone and left my baby, and now I'm sad and blue.*

Really, Kate had no idea where this stuff came from.

"Two words for you, Katie," her dad said, and now he was grinning like a maniac as he pulled out his wallet and waved the waitress over to their table. "Free. Bird. 'Free Bird.' Do you know that song? Man, I love Lynyrd Skynyrd! I've got their greatest hits CD in my car."

Kate started to giggle. She'd never seen her dad like this before. "I like Lynyrd Skynyrd too. I could listen to some Lynyrd Skynyrd and drive around with you."

"And play some hoops?" Mr. Faber asked, sounding hopeful. "I think you'd feel better if you did."

"Okay, okay!" Kate said, still giggling. When the waitress came back to their table with her Danish, she wrapped it in a napkin and slid out of the booth to follow her dad through the restaurant's din and out to the parking lot.

"You'll see," Mr. Faber said, opening the passenger-side door for her. "You're going to feel so much better after this."

"Maybe," Kate said. "But maybe I'll feel worse."

"Wait and see," her dad said. "Wait and see."

Kate got into the car and started nibbling her Danish, and that definitely made her feel better. She guessed she might feel okay in a little while. She didn't feel too terrible right now. Even though there was still sadness inside of her, she could feel something light, too. Maybe it was a bird that had just discovered it was free, she thought. Maybe it was a bird about to fly.

the light you can hold in your hands

On Saturday morning Marylin wakes to the sound of chattering, and when she opens her eyes, she sees a bird sitting on her window-sill chirping away, like it's trying to tell her something. *Wake up!* Or *Spring is here!* Or *This is the first Saturday of the rest of your life!*

Marylin likes the idea of a bird waking her up. Didn't that happen in *Snow White*? Or maybe it was *Cinderella*. A little bluebird, or a flock of bluebirds, chirping cheerfully, flying around a bed with a garland of flowers. Something like that.

"A flock of bluebirds chirping cheerfully," Marylin says out loud as she kicks off the sheets.

Maybe that could be her mantra, the phrase she repeats to herself over and over like a magic spell to ward off bad thoughts. She had one of her cheerleading nightmares again last night, the one where she was on top of the pyramid, balanced on Caitlin's and Mazie's backs, when suddenly the whole thing collapsed and she went flying into the stands. "Somebody catch me," she called out in her dream, but everyone was too busy scrambling to get out of the way, even Kate, even Benjamin.

A flock of bluebirds chirping cheerfully, she thinks as she stretches her arms over her legs and grabs her toes. And then she thinks, Kate would try to catch me. She'd never move out of the way.

Benjamin? She's not so sure. He's been acting funny lately. He *did* ask her to the spring dance, but he doesn't seem all that excited about it. Is it really possible he cares that she quit cheerleading? How could that be? She's still the same person, after all. Her situation may have changed, but she hasn't.

Marylin pushes away the thought that maybe

everything would be fine if she hadn't tried to make Benjamin get the cheerleaders new uniforms. She can't stand the thought that she might have ruined their relationship. She'd rather think that Benjamin thought it was cool dating a cheerleader, and now he's less interested. So what if that seems unlikely? So what if Benjamin seems like the last person in the world to think that way?

A flock of bluebirds chirping cheerfully. A flock of bluebirds chirping cheerfully.

So. Anyway. What does she want to do today? If Marylin were still a cheerleader, she'd already be on the bus headed for the boys' basketball game across town, but she's a civilian now, and she can do whatever she wants all day long.

It is, Marylin has to admit as she pulls on her bathrobe, a little depressing. No! Not depressing. She will not be depressed. However, she can admit that it feels sort of weird not to have her whole day laid out for her. She can admit that her closet seems empty since she donated her cheerleading uniform to Goodwill. But she refuses to think any thoughts that aren't positive. She has a whole day to herself! She'll make a to-do list, she decides, filled with fun, fabulous activities.

Number one on her list, she decides, will be dealing with her room, which suddenly strikes her as boring. She'll call Rhetta, and together they can work on a room makeover. A post-cheerleading room makeover. Maybe Marylin can get her mom to drive them to Everything But Granny's Panties, a consignment shop where they sell old stuff that you can fix up. Marylin would like a new desk; the one she has now is too small, and it doesn't have any personality.

Marylin decides that creating a room with personality is her number one priority today. Then she smiles and goes downstairs, happy that her life now has a purpose.

Her mom is sitting at the table eating a bagel when Marylin walks into the kitchen. "I thought you weren't doing carbs anymore," Marylin says, opening the fridge. "Did you change your mind?"

Her mom sighs. "No, not really. But what's life without bagels?"

"Boring," Marylin agrees. She grabs some string cheese and an apple and sits down across from her mom. "Almost as boring as life without pizza."

"Life without pizza is not worth living," Marylin's mom says, checking her watch and sighing again. "Petey's got a birthday party this afternoon, which naturally I forgot all about, and now I've got to go to Target and get something. I can't wait for the birthday party years to be over. I feel like I spend half my time in Target buying presents for Petey's classmates."

"I bet there's something in Petey's closet you can regift," Marylin says, peeling the wrapper off her string cheese. "Didn't he get two of the same Lego kits for Christmas? You said you were going to return one, but there wasn't a gift receipt."

Her mom's eyes light up. "Yes! That architecture kit—he got two Guggenheim Museums. Marylin, you're a genius!"

"We're starting a reuse, reduce, recycle

campaign at school," Marylin tells her mom. "Student Government is, I mean. Maybe we should make it 'reuse, reduce, recycle, and regift.'"

"You're joking, but that's a great idea." Her mom pushes her chair away from the table and stands. "We've got so much stuff we never use. I mean, I have at least three blow dryers, and one of them's practically new. Maybe that's what I'll give to Aunt Tish for her birthday."

"Just make sure there aren't any hairs sticking out of it," Marylin says. "It's one thing to get a used blow dryer for your birthday; it's another thing to get a hairy used blow dryer."

"Point taken," her mom tells her. "Okay, I'm off to find the funny pages, which I'm going to recycle into wrapping paper."

Marylin takes a bite out of her apple and checks the clock. Eight thirty. The day stretches out in front of her. Except now that she's decided that her room is her number one priority, things are starting to take shape in her mind. She needs to take inventory of her stuff, and she definitely needs to clean out her closet. Anything that doesn't make her heart sing goes to Goodwill.

Her mom's phone rings from across the table, and Marylin reaches over to grab it. When she sees her dad's number on the screen, she hits the talk button.

"Hey, Dad, it's me," she says through a mouthful of apple. "Mom's wrapping a present."

"Don't tell me," her dad says, laughing. "Petey's got another birthday party."

"This afternoon," Marylin confirms. "I think it's at the Museum of Life and Science, so he's probably thrilled."

"Well, tell your mom I'm going to be over that way around four. I'd be happy to pick him up, if that would help."

An idea comes to Marylin so suddenly she practically flips over her chair. "You know what would be a big help? If you could pick up Petey from the party, and then you guys could get some pizza and bring it home for dinner."

She squeezes her eyes shut. Please, please, please, she thinks. Her dad had dinner with them on Christmas Eve, and it was practically the best night of her life. Better than when she made the cheerleading squad, and almost as good as the day Benjamin came over and built snowmen with her and Petey. No, even better than that.

"Marylin," her dad says, his voice soft. "I don't want you to—"

But he doesn't finish his sentence. All of a sudden there is a string of silence between Marylin and her dad. A garland of silence, she thinks, imagining a bluebird perched on her dad's shoulder and another one hovering over her mom's phone, each holding on to its end of the quiet.

"Just because you and Mom aren't married anymore doesn't mean we're not a family," Marylin says after what seems like a million years. "You're still our dad, Mom is still our mom. And it doesn't even seem like you guys hate each other anymore."

"We don't hate each other," Mr. McIntosh agrees. "We never hated each other." He pauses. "Okay, maybe we hated each other for five minutes."

"I think it will be better for my wedding day if you guys are friends," Marylin insists.

Her father laughs. "When did the invitations go out? I didn't know you were getting married."

"Not now, but one day," Marylin says, and she imagines walking down the aisle toward a taller, older-looking Benjamin Huddle, a flock of bluebirds carrying the train of her dress. "And I don't want any broken-family drama."

Her dad laughs again. "Okay, I'll tell you what. Let me talk to your mom and get her take on this."

Marylin finds her mom in her bedroom, taping up the Guggenheim Museum. "Can Dad come over to dinner tonight if he picks up Petey from the party?"

Marylin's mom looks surprised, then relieved. "If Dad picks up Petey, he can come over for dinner every Saturday night for the next month. I hate driving over to Life and Science from here on Saturday. It takes forever."

"Tell him that!" Marylin says, handing her mom the phone. "I'm going to go get dressed."

She closes her mom's bedroom door behind her but stands in the hall for a moment, listening. Her mom's voice is muffled, but it's friendly, cheerful even.

A flock of bluebirds chirping cheerfully, Marylin thinks, and then she wonders if she has anything orange to wear. It is one of Marylin's gifts that she looks good in orange, especially if it's a peachy-orange. Maybe when she and Rhetta go to Everything But Granny's Panties, they can look for vintage clothes. Reuse, Reduce, Recycle, that's Marylin's new motto, after all.

Can you recycle your family? she wonders as she walks down the hallway to her room. Can you recycle your life?

She thinks maybe you can. She thinks maybe she'll give it a try.

Matthew Holler wakes up at 10:37 on Saturday morning and tries to go back to sleep, but he can't. He's too psyched. Today he's getting together with Bob Stockfish and Jackson Hill in Bob's garage, and if everything works out, it's going to be the beginning of the most totally awesome band that ever was.

Matthew grabs a T-shirt from the floor next to his bed, pulls it on, and then grabs his guitar. He plays first thing every day, partly because playing guitar is his favorite thing to do, and partly to remind himself what his priorities are. Number one: music. Number two: Well, he's not quite sure about number two. He knows it ought to be school, but it's not. He knows he's supposed to be this great student— he's supposedly gifted or something—but as soon as he walks into the building, it's like his brain falls asleep. The only place he feels really alive at school is in the audio lab. If he could spend all day there, he'd definitely be a happy camper.

Maybe he doesn't have a second priority. Maybe music is it. Well, there are his friends, sure. There's Kate. But Kate's complicated. He knows she likes him, even though she tries to act like she doesn't. And sometimes he feels like—well, he doesn't know what he feels like. Like he wouldn't mind hanging out with her all the time. Before she told him to back off, some-times he went over to her house just because he wanted to be in the same part of the universe with her. But then she'd give him this look, this *I'm really into you* look, and Matthew wanted to be a million miles away. Like he was really mad at her or something. And then five minutes later, he wanted to hold her hand. It made him feel crazy.

You're an idiot, he tells himself. You sound like a no-brain romance novel. This is why he has music. *Needs* music. It gets him away from himself and all his stupid feelings. He doesn't know anything; he just feels a lot of random feelings that push him here and there. Why even think about it? Why even try to figure it out?

He starts working on a riff from the new Wilco song he heard last night on K-DUCK and immediately downloaded off of iTunes. It's a noisy song, like a lot of Wilco's stuff, and Matthew's definitely into noise. Not just any kind of noise, though. What he likes are melo-dies that are covered up with cacophony, pretty songs you can hardly hear over the buzzing and the echoes and loud rushes of wind. But the melody has to be there. There's got to be a song at the heart of all the noise. The noise has to be covering something up.

It's like the melody's a secret, he thinks. And the noise keeps the secret safe.

That's when it occurs to him what his real priority needs to be: getting an electric guitar. Talk about noise, he thinks. Talk about a wall of sound.

He leans back against his pillow, still strumming, imagining himself playing electric guitar in front of a huge stack of amplifiers. He imagines the rush of power surging through his arms, down through his hands and into the guitar before it crashes over the horde of screaming fans in front of him. Behind him, Jackson's pounding the drums so that the whole thing's practically tribal, and Bob's screaming into the mic, the words all distorted and wild.

Matthew shakes his head and smiles. How awesome would that be? He definitely needs his dad to give him a ride over to Slim's Guitar

World before lunch. What would a used Fender go for? Like five hundred dollars? A thousand? Not that Matthew's got that kind of dough, but maybe he can get a job mowing lawns or something. He could borrow the money from his parents and pay them back.

Man, he wants to call Kate! Because she would totally get this, totally understand why he needs to go electric right this very minute. She started out on electric, which kills him. How cool is that? Really, he ought to be in a band with Kate, that's what he ought to do. She writes awesome songs, for one thing. And she gets music, how it's the most important thing.

Matthew glances over at his desk, where his cell is sitting on a pile of junk. It's been over a week since Kate asked him to leave her alone. That's long enough, right? She's definitely proven she doesn't care anymore—she hasn't stopped by the audio lab or written him any notes; she even skipped Creative Writing Club this week. So it should be okay to call, right?

He starts to lean over to grab the phone, but stops himself. Better idea: He'll wait a week and then call her and see if she wants to come to watch band practice. What's Ms. Vickery always saying in Creative Writing Club? Show, don't tell? Matthew will show Kate how cool being in a band is. He'll show her how cool *he* is.

He'll show Kate how much she's missing him, and then maybe she'll come back.

Petey McIntosh still has dreams of being a spy, but he thinks now he'd like to be the kind of spy who talks to people and gets their deep dark secrets out of them. An interrogator kind of spy. So now, in the car with his dad, a bag of party favors in his lap, he decides he's going to get to the bottom of the story. Why exactly is his dad coming to dinner?

"So how are you and Mom getting along these days?" Petey asks as they turn onto Roxboro Road. He tries to sound casual, like he's making small talk at a party. "Seems like you're communicating a little more than you used to."

His dad gives him a startled look. "Uh, you know, fine. I've always been—uh—very fond of your mom."

"That's probably why you married her," Petey says, nodding.

His dad nods back but doesn't elaborate. "Why don't we listen to a CD?" Mr. McIntosh suggests after a moment. "Name your poison."

"Do you have the new Paul Simon CD?" Petey asks. "Mom really likes it. Except it's not really a CD, since she got it on iTunes. Last night at dinner we were trying to figure out what do you call a CD that's not actually a CD you can hold in your hands. Marylin said maybe you call it a playlist, but me and Mom thought that sounded weird. 'How do you like the new Paul Simon playlist?' It doesn't sound right."

"I don't know what to call anything these days," his dad replies amiably, pulling into Woodcroft Shopping Center. "Book on tape or audiobook? Who knows anymore?"

"Audiobook," Petey says. "Everybody knows that."

"Everybody *your* age knows that," his dad says, parking the car in front of Pulcinella's, where they're going to pick up their pizzas.

"You've grown up in a world devoid of cassette tapes. But for people my age, it's more confusing."

Petey waits in the car while his dad goes inside to get the pizzas. It's interesting to look at his dad like he's a stranger. How would he describe him to the police? Tall, kind of skinny, messy clothes. Even when his dad is dressed up to go someplace important, a big meeting or a conference, there's always something out of whack. His shirts don't stay tucked in, his ties are off center, his shoes need polishing. Today Petey's dad is dressed pretty casually, so there's not too much that can go wrong, but some of the hair on the back of his head is sticking out, like he forgot to comb it, which he probably did.

Petey checks out his treat bag to see if there's any candy in it. Hardly anybody's mom puts candy in treat bags; mostly it's just pencils and animal-shaped erasers that don't really work. But every once in a while you get lucky. You get a mom like Seth Halladay's, whose treat bags are famous all over the fourth grade for being filled with full-size Snickers bars and Pixy Stix.

There's nothing to eat in today's treat bag except astronaut ice cream, which is just freeze-dried something, and in Petey's opinion, tastes awful. He'll take it to school on Monday to see if he can trade it for something good. He wonders if Marylin likes astronaut ice cream, and then he wonders if there's anything Marylin has that he'd like to trade for. Probably not. Marylin keeps some candy in her room—Petey knows this because he checks out her drawers every once in a while, a strictly spy-related maneuver, nothing personal—but it's stuff he doesn't like very much, like Skittles, which to Petey are just second-rate M&Ms.

Now that he thinks about it, Petey hasn't done one of his spy maneuvers in Marylin's room since she quit cheerleading. She's there a lot more now, usually with her friend Rhetta, who Petey likes okay, though not as much as he likes Kate. Kate is Petey's dream woman. Smart, athletic, pretty, and nice to fourth-grade boys. And now she plays guitar and wears cool black boots. Petey hopes she'll be in a famous band someday and invite him backstage at one of her concerts. He thinks if he's friends with a famous person, maybe Collin Waits will quit calling him Geek Boy and trying to push him off the monkey bars at recess.

Petey's last spy maneuver was when Ruby and Mazie came over so Marylin could tell them she was quitting the cheerleading squad. Petey stood as still as he could outside of Marylin's room, his ear to the door. He'd read somewhere that you should keep your friends close and your enemies closer. He'd immediately thought of Mazie, who was the worst friend Marylin had ever had, in Petey's opinion.

"We're not doctors who make house calls," Mazie said. "Why don't you tell us why we just *had* to come over? Like we don't have anything better to do than to come to your house— which smells, by the way. You need to get your carpets cleaned."

Marylin ignored this, but Petey sniffed the air a few times to see if he could tell what Mazie was talking about. The house smelled fine to him. It always smelled fine. That Mazie must be crazy.

"I just wanted to let you know in person that I've decided to leave my position as cheerleader," Marylin said. Petey liked how she sounded very professional, like someone on TV.

"Your what?" Mazie's voice got all snarly—or at least, snarlier. "Your position? What do you think this is, a law firm?"

"You know what I mean."

The other girl, Ruby, said, "You mean you're quitting the squad? Do you think we really care?"

"I guess I thought you might. I mean, the routines will have to be changed. Nobody else can do a double back walkover, for one thing."

Ruby laughed. "Believe me, Marylin—you're replaceable."

"Highly replaceable," Mazie added.

There was a pause, and then Marylin said, "Anyway, I already told Coach Wells, and she was totally understanding about it. I hope you will be too. It's just right now, I've got so much going on, and I'm sort of worried about my grades—"

"Face it, Marylin," Mazie interrupted her. "We win. We wanted you gone, and now you're going."

The problem with being a spy, Petey thought, was that you had to keep your feelings out of it. If he weren't observing the spy code, he would have busted through the door right then and there and socked Mazie in the nose. What a rotten human being!

"You're wrong," Marylin replied quietly. "I'm the one who wins, because I don't have to live by your rules anymore. Anyway, we're done here. You can go now."

"Come on, Mazie, this is stupid. If Marylin wants to ruin her life, let her."

Petey scurried into the bathroom before the door opened and he was discovered. He stood there in the dark, his heart pounding so loud in his ears he was sure everyone in the house could hear it.

A few minutes later, Marylin opened the bathroom door and found Petey standing in the dark. "What are you doing?" she asked.

"Just thinking."

"In the bathroom?"

"I do some of my best thinking here."

"Well, why don't you think about setting the

table before Mom gets home from work?" Marylin suggested. "If we get done eating early, maybe we'll have time to go get ice cream after dinner."

Petey wanted to tell Marylin that he was proud of her for standing up to Ruby and Mazie, but he couldn't. That would be breaking the spy code, and Petey never broke the spy code. Instead he said, "I'm glad you're around more now. It's more fun when you're here."

Marylin gave him a strange look, but then she smiled. "It's nice to be home."

Petey thinks about this now as he looks out the car window and sees his dad coming back with the pizzas, which they are taking home to eat like a regular family. Petey prepares himself for the unbelievable torture of riding in the car with right-out-of-the-oven-hot-pizza smell. Somebody should bottle that smell, Petey thinks. Someone should sell it like perfume.

"So, man to man, how do you think Marylin's doing these days?" his dad asks after he's put the pizza in the backseat and started up the car again. "You think she's okay?"

Petey thinks about this. "Well, she definitely seems happier than she did when she was still a cheerleader. She hardly ever cries anymore. But I think she sort of misses it. Being a cheer-leader, I mean."

"Do you think she's unhappy?" his dad asks, sounding worried.

Petey shrugs. "She's got a boyfriend, and she's got friends. Kate comes over sometimes now, but she and Marylin are always arguing about stuff. Last time she was over, Kate was talking about getting a crew cut. I thought Marylin was going to have a cow."

His dad laughs and says, "Old Kate. She's a good egg."

She's a great egg, Petey thinks. And then he remembers he's on a mission. He leans back casually, tapping his fingers against the win-dow, la la la, nobody here but us chickens. "So, you're staying for dinner, right?"

"Your mom invited me," his dad says. "We both think it's a good idea for the four of us to do something together every once in a while. As your sister pointed out to me today on the phone, we'll always be a family, right?"

"Right," Petey agrees, deciding not to add that they'd be even more of a family if his mom and dad stopped being divorced. Petey likes to be more subtle than that.

As soon as the car pulls into the driveway, Marylin rushes out to meet them. Either she's really hungry, Petey thinks, or else she's got some big news. Did their mom finally agree to let them get a dog?

"Well, she sure looks happy right now, doesn't she, Pete?" his dad asks, and Petey nods. He likes it when his dad calls him Pete. He sits up a little straighter in his seat. One day he's going to be tall like his dad, and then Collin Waits better watch out.

"Come see my room!" Marylin calls as Petey and his dad get out of the car. "Rhetta and I worked on it all afternoon, and it's perfect. Except that it needs paint. Could you take me to Lowe's after dinner to get some paint, Dad? I was thinking a really light yellow with just a touch of orange in it. A totally light peachy color. And maybe you could help me paint tomorrow? Because Mom's no fun to paint with. She's too nit picky."

Petey sees his dad hesitate and wonders what the big deal is. Is it because his dad doesn't live in their house? Is there something weird about painting a room in a house that used to be yours but isn't anymore?

"Maybe, honey, we'll see," his dad says, which as far as Petey is concerned is Parent Talk for "no."

"Please, Daddy?" Marylin says, coming over to Mr. McIntosh and grabbing his arm, so that he almost drops the pizza he's carrying. "It's really important to me. Really, really important."

"Yeah, please, Dad," somebody else says, and Petey's surprised to realize that it's him. He's the one holding on to his dad's other arm. And he's even more surprised to realize that he's the one who's about to cry.

I'm going to be really tall someday and everything will be fine, Petey tells himself to make the tears go away. He stands up super straight. "I'll help," he says to his dad. "It would only take a couple of hours."

"We better get inside before this pizza gets cold," Mr. McIntosh says. "Your mom hates cold pizza."

Petey follows his dad and Marylin inside the house. It's hard work being a spy, he thinks. The world is full of secrets and danger. All you can do is observe and ask questions. All you can do is try to get to the bottom of things.

"Hey, Mom," he calls out as he walks into the kitchen. "How do you like Dad's shirt? Pretty nice, huh?"

His mom glances over at his dad. "Well, since I gave your dad that shirt, I guess I like it a lot. He always looks nice in it."

"He's a handsome guy," Petey agrees. He looks at Marylin, and she looks at him. Petey bets she's thinking the same thing he is. She's thinking there might be hope after all. Maybe that's a mistake and they should believe their parents when they say they're not going to get married again. That they're happy just being friends.

Maybe. But Petey would rather hope for something bigger. He'd rather hope that one day his parents will live in the same house again. They don't even have to get remarried. Petey doesn't care. He just wants everyone together, like a family that doesn't have to keep saying, "We're still a family."

He wants to be a part of a family that knows it's a family without ever having to say a word.

When Kate used to play basketball, her favorite part of the game was after it was over, when she felt all used up in a good way. She'd take a shower, put on clean clothes, and notice how good clean clothes felt, fresh and cool against her skin, the light scent of the fabric sheets her mom used just barely there but nice. After a game, whatever she put in her mouth tasted amazing, chips, pizza, spaghetti, it didn't matter. Her body hummed with the happiness of having spent sixty minutes stretching and jumping and sprinting up and down the court a hundred times.

And now, sitting on the roof outside her bedroom window after band practice, she feels the same way. Like she's had the best workout of her life. Like her muscles have been uploading oxygen all afternoon.

Kate has just started roof sitting. She got the idea from a comic strip where a teenage boy sits on his roof a lot and thinks about stuff. One day, walking home from the bus stop, Kate realized she could do the same thing—that it would be easy to slip out of her bedroom window onto the part of the roof that overhung the front porch. So now she's a roof sitter, and she thinks she'll always be a roof sitter, because, as it turns out, her roof is the best place in the world to get away from everyone and do some real thinking.

What she wants to think about now is band practice. Two days ago it never occurred to her that she could be in a band, and then yesterday, Friday, this girl named Torie Reisman came over to where Kate was digging raised beds in the student commons garden and said, "Hey, I heard that you play guitar. My dad just said I could use his drum kit out in the garage, so I'm trying to get some kids to come over and jam tomorrow. You up for it?"

Kate didn't even *know* Torie Reisman. Well,

she knew who Torie was, seventh grader, pretty smart, computer lab rat, jeans and T-shirt, hair always pulled back in a ponytail. Kate never would have guessed she was also the kind of person who would have a drum kit in her garage.

"Uh, yeah, sure." Kate straightened up and brushed the dirt off her hands. "Although I guess I should ask what kind of music you want to play."

"I'm still figuring that out," Torie told her. "I'm sort of into the music my dad likes, just because he plays it all the time in the car. Like, the Rolling Stones and Bruce Springsteen and stuff? But I also—I don't know. I mean, I just got an iPod? So I've been downloading all kinds of songs, and I kind of like everything. So I'm open."

"Cool," Kate said. "Have you ever played drums before?"

Torie shook her head and grinned. "Never. But I heard you're pretty good on guitar. And this girl Carter Ricks, who lives in my neighborhood? She's homeschooled? She plays stand-up bass in her family's old-time band. She said electric bass would be no problem, though."

"I've only got an acoustic guitar," Kate told her. "But my friend has an electric one I could probably use."

"You can rock out on acoustic," Torie said. "You just have to use a pickup. We'll figure it out. I've been reading my dad's old *Musician* magazines and learning tons of stuff. My mom's always bugging him to throw 'em out, but he won't. He calls them 'the expressway to his youth,' whatever that means."

So Saturday morning Kate got up and went to *Guys and Dolls* rehearsal, and then after lunch she got her dad to drive her over to Torie's house. Carter Ricks was already there, sitting on an overturned milk crate and plucking out notes on a red bass guitar. "It's weird to be sitting down while I play," she said when Kate walked in, not bothering to introduce herself first. "There's a reason they call a stand-up bass a stand-up bass."

"I thought there might be," Kate replied, setting down her guitar case. "But it's nice to know for sure."

Just then Torie came out of the house, a pair of drumsticks in one hand, a MacBook in the other. "You know we're going to sound awful today, right?"

Carter shrugged. "Maybe. But sometimes even awful sounds good."

And they did sound pretty awful at first. They decided to learn how to play the Rolling Stones song "Satisfaction," since it was a song they all knew. They listened to it on iTunes a couple of times, and took a look at some chord charts they pulled up on the Internet. "Let's give it a go," Torie finally declared. "No time like the present, etc., etc."

"You know, I don't think 'Satisfaction' is the right choice for this outfit," Carter said after the fifth time they'd tried and totally failed to play something resembling the song they'd been listening to. "Do you guys know this band called Midtown Dickens? They get played a lot on K-DUCK. They have this really cool, pared-down thing going on that might really work for us."

That's when Kate knew she and Carter were definitely going to be friends. By the end of the afternoon, they'd gotten the song "Only Brother" pretty much down and were in agreement that they could use a banjo player. Kate liked how her and Carter's voices fit together, weaving over and under each other. It was fun singing with someone else, she realized. Fun to make music in somebody's garage, the sound of kids playing baseball down the street, bats cracking, voices crying out "I got it!" floating through the songs. It was like being on a team, Kate thought during a break as she sipped on the Coke that Torie had grabbed out of the garage fridge. The coolest team in the world.

Now she stretches out her arms to the darkening sky and sings, "*I am my only brother, but this cavern is not my home. . . .*"

She lets herself think about band practice a little more, holding off for a minute the next thing she wants to think about, something she doesn't want to ruin by overthinking it. Finally, though, she gives in and thinks about Matthew Holler.

After band practice, her dad stopped at the Quick-E Mart to pick up a quart of milk, and

Kate went in with him, just to look around. You never knew what you might find at the Quick-E Mart. Once Kate had bought a pack of six glow-in-the-dark mechanical pencils for ninety-nine cents, and another time she'd gotten a copy of *Wonder Woman* in Chinese. She'd taken it in for show-and-tell, and this kid named Sonio Lee, who came from Hong Kong, translated it for the class.

While her dad was waiting in line, Kate had scurried to the magazine rack. Maybe she'd find the latest issue of *Rolling Stone* or *Guitar Player*. Instead what she found was Matthew Holler.

"Whoa," he'd said when he saw her. "I was just thinking about you." He held out a copy of *Guitar World*. "There's an article on electric guitar gods who started out as acoustic guitarists, and I was thinking they should do one on acoustic players who started out on electric."

Kate couldn't hold back. "I just had my first band practice! I mean, just this very minute. Do you know Torie Reisman? We practiced at her house."

Matthew took a step back, a big smile blooming across his face. "Dude, I just had band practice too. Over at Bob Stockfish's. It totally rocked, except for the part where we stunk up the joint."

"Us too!" Kate exclaimed. "At first I thought, This is never going to work. But then we kind of figured it out."

"Kate?" Mr. Faber stood at the end of the aisle. "Oh, hi, Matthew. Good to see you."

"Hey, Mr. Faber," Matthew said. "Kate and I were just talking about music."

"As usual," Mr. Faber said, and then he checked his watch. "I'll be in the car, Kate. Five minutes, okay?"

Kate looked at Matthew, and they both grinned, like old friends who hadn't seen each other in years. "Okay," she said. "Five minutes. What can we accomplish in five minutes?"

"We could talk about the good old days," Matthew suggested.

"Let's talk about band practice instead," Kate told him. So they went to stand in line so Matthew could pay for his magazine, and they talked about their bands. They talked about whether Kate should put a pickup on her guitar or if Carter could just keep her amp low, and they talked about how much it would cost to rent practice space at the community center, because Matthew could tell Bob's mom was not into the idea of having band practice at her house on a regular basis.

They walked out of the store, still talking, and stood at the bagged ice freezer, where they suddenly stopped talking and just stared at each other, both of them looking awkward and tense.

"I guess I ought to get going," Kate said finally. "Do you need a ride?"

"Nah, there's a shortcut to my house around back." Matthew rolled up his magazine and slipped it into his back pocket. "But maybe you could come over sometime? Like tomorrow?"

Kate wanted to say yes. She missed Matthew. A lot. But she wasn't ready to give up the feeling she'd gotten that afternoon, playing with Torie and Carter, this feeling of being strong and free and, well, *alive*. If she started hanging out with Matthew again, she might lose it. She might trade it in for the feeling of having an almost boyfriend.

"Maybe not tomorrow," she said after a minute. "But sometime, okay? I mean, soon. Like maybe when the play's over. Are you coming to it, by the way? Opening night is next Friday."

"Sure," Matthew said. "Sounds good." He reached out his hand, as though he were going to touch Kate's hair, but then seemed to think maybe that wasn't a great idea and shoved it into his pocket instead. "I'll see you then. And we'll hang out together soon, definitely."

He turned to leave, and Kate turned to leave, and just as she reached the car, Matthew called out, "That's awesome about the band, Kate."

Kate looked at him. "It's awesome about your band too. You'll be great."

Matthew nodded, and then he went around the corner of the store and was gone. Kate stood by the car door for another second, looking at the empty space he had left behind him. *Come back,* she wanted to call, but she didn't. Because as much as she wanted Matthew Holler, there were other things she wanted more.

• • •

"What on earth are you doing out here?" Kate's dad sticks his head out of the window. "You're going to break your arm. Or get pneumonia."

"Maybe both," Kate says pleasantly. "Plus rabies, if there are any raccoons up here."

Mr. Faber climbs through the window and sits down next to Kate. "Aren't you freezing?"

"I've got a sweater on," Kate points out. "And it's not that cold. It's going to be spring soon."

"In a couple of weeks, maybe. It still might snow. So, was band practice fun?"

Kate shrugs. Sometimes she doesn't know how to answer her dad's questions. He's always asking if things were fun. Was school fun today? Was PE fun today? Did you have fun spending the night at Marylin's? Kate's thirteen; her life really isn't about fun anymore. It's about bigger things now.

"It was good," Kate tells her dad. "Only at first it was terrible. It took us a while to figure out how to play together."

"I had some roommates in college who were in a band," her dad says. "I used to watch them practice, and the first twenty minutes were always worthless."

Kate leans back against the roof and looks up at the stars. It's still early, so there aren't a ton, but she can see one or two, plus the moon. *One or two stars plus the moon.* Her mind goes to work on this, trying to turn it into a song—*One or two stars, the moon and you.* No, definitely not right. *Two stars and a lonely moon, another night here without you.* Better. When she goes back inside, she'll write it down, play around with it some more.

"I heard you singing just now. It sounded nice," her dad says. "You get that from your mom. I can't sing a note."

"I practice a lot. It helps."

Her dad nods. "It's the key to everything, practicing. I used to think you were either naturally good at something or you weren't. I was a terrible runner when I was a kid, really slow, and I thought I'd never get any better. But I knew I'd never make the JV basketball team if I couldn't run, so the summer before ninth grade I got up at six every morning and ran as fast as I could up and down our street for thirty minutes. Totally wore myself out."

"Did it work?"

"Yeah, I got a lot faster. Not like I was the fastest guy in the ninth grade, but I got fast enough to make JV anyway."

Kate wonders what she needs to practice. Singing harmonies and learning how to pick the guitar instead of just strum, definitely. She should probably practice being nicer to Tracie, although it's hard to be nice to someone who never replaces the toilet paper when she finishes up a roll and always takes the last piece of cake without asking if anyone else wants it.

Not missing Matthew Holler—that's something she's been practicing for over a week now, and she's getting a little bit better at it, but she's still not an expert. She knows she was right today to tell Matthew she couldn't hang out with him yet. But she hopes more than anything that one day she'll be able to be friends with him and not want to kiss him every second.

"*You're the man of my dreams, you're the man in the moon,*" she sings, forgetting that her dad is sitting right next to her.

"Thanks, Katie," he says, grinning. "I didn't know you cared."

Kate is quiet for a minute, focusing on the brightest spot in the sky, wondering if it's a star or a planet. Maybe it's Venus, the evening star. She likes that—a planet being called a star, one thing being called the opposite thing. But are stars and planets opposites? She's not sure. How about stars and moons?

This is why she likes sitting on the roof. You never know what thoughts are going to come into your head, which direction your mind will go in. Maybe during the summer, she'll sleep out here, under the moon, and dream all sorts of crazy dreams.

"I care too much," she says, breaking the silence. "That's the problem. But I'm trying not to. I'm practicing how not to care."

"Don't," Mr. Faber says, and to Kate's surprise, his voice is sharp. "That's the worst thing in the world you can do."

Then they're both quiet, and Kate realizes suddenly that she doesn't really know her dad all that well. He's just her dad to her, not a real person, not someone who might have some experience when it comes to caring too much.

Kate reaches over and puts her hand on her dad's, just for a second. Just long enough to let him know she'll never be able to stop caring, no matter how much she practices.

"What are you guys doing out there?" Tracie's face appears at Kate's window. She pokes her head out and makes a face, like something on the roof stinks. "It's freezing!"

"Just having a heart-to-heart," Mr. Faber tells her. "Want to join us?"

Tracie barks a sharp laugh. "Yeah, right. Mom said to tell you the pizza's on its way. She hopes everyone's okay with one veggie and one pepperoni and mushroom."

"Fine by me," Mr. Faber says. "How about you, Katie?"

Kate nods, and Tracie pulls her head back inside. "It's freezing!" she says again, and then she slams down the window.

Mr. Faber turns and looks at Kate. "You know these windows don't open from the outside, don't you?"

Kate shakes her head in dismay. "Right now I'm practicing not hating Tracie's guts."

"Well, I'm practicing being brave enough to climb down off the roof," her dad says. "It's not that far to the ground, but I'd hate to fall."

"We could just wait until the pizza guy gets here and yell at him to tell Mom," Kate suggests. "It won't be that long."

Her dad thinks about this for a second and nods his head. "Sure, okay."

So Kate and her dad sit on the roof, not really talking, mostly just thinking their own thoughts, and Kate decides it's kind of nice, sitting on the roof with someone else, looking out at the stars. She scootches a little closer to her dad, but not all the way close. She needs a little space between her and other people, space to fit in the music and the poems and the crazy dreams that belong to her and no one else. But she needs the closeness, too. This is what she has to figure out. How do you have both? How do you have the caring and the not caring too much, the kiss good night and the walk home alone?

It's like the stars, she thinks. The faraway

stars and the light you can hold in your hands. You need them both, one to look at, the other to help you see. Something like that. Kate knows she's going to have to think about this some more before she gets it all figured out. That's okay. She's got time.

She shivers, and her dad asks, "You cold?"

"A little," she admits. "But the pizza guy will be here soon."

And sure enough, she sees the car at the end of the street, with its little triangle of light on top, driving in their direction. She's almost sorry to see him, even if she is getting cold. There's so much she needs to think about, like whether she should save up for an electric guitar, and if they should ask more people to join the band, and when it's going to be time to be friends with Matthew Holler again.

Pretty soon, she thinks. Not too long from now. She needs a little more time to practice caring without caring too much. To practice holding the light in her hands. To practice letting it go.

ACKNOWLEDGMENTS

The author would like to thank Caitlyn Dlouhy, the brains of this operation, and Ariel Colletti, who is as lovely as her name. Thanks to Justin Chanda for his ongoing and unwavering support and for just being a great guy.

Thanks to Valerie Shea, genius copy editor; eagle-eye production editor Kaitlin Severini; Sonia Chaghatzbanian and Michael McCartney, who design such beautiful books; and production manager Chava Wolin, who makes it all come out right.

As always, this author would be at a loss without her fine friends to keep her sane. Special thanks go to Lisa Brown, Amy Graham, Sandy Hasenauer, Jaye Lapachet, and Sarah Schulz in this regard. Many thanks to the good people at Pretty fab PR, who throw pretty fab book parties, and to the folks at Flyleaf Books in Chapel Hill. Thank you, Stephanie Rosen, for being an ideal reader, and to your mom, Michelle Rosen, for being an ideal librarian.

As always, the author would like to acknowledge Clifton, Jack, and Will Dowell, the most awesome family a girl could ask for, and Travis, her dog, who kept her company while she wrote this book.